He couldn't help himself.

Rick shifted just enough to pull her close for a kiss. If felt good. It felt right and real. Maggie was sweet to taste and warm to touch.

He had just enough sense to let Maggie go before he couldn't let her go at all. Stiffly, he straightened in his seat. She straightened, too, putting distance between them. She didn't look angry. Just…dazed.

"I've been wanting to do that for a while," he said.

"So have I."

That caught him by surprise.

"But it's not going to happen again. Distractions like that can cost a life. We'd best get going," she said. She looked at him as if daring him to protest. Rick couldn't help noticing that her fingers were trembling.

"Right." He shoved the gearshift into Drive.

He was half a mile down the road before he thought to ask where it was they were going.

Dear Reader,

Once again, Silhouette Intimate Moments has a month's worth of fabulous reading for you. Start by picking up *Wanted,* the second in Ruth Langan's suspenseful DEVIL'S COVE miniseries. This small town is full of secrets, and this top-selling author knows how to keep readers turning the pages.

We have more terrific miniseries. Kathleen Creighton continues STARRS OF THE WEST with *An Order of Protection,* featuring a protective hero every reader will want to have on her side. In *Joint Forces,* Catherine Mann continues WINGMEN WARRIORS with Tag's long-awaited story. Seems Tag and his wife are also awaiting something: the unexpected arrival of another child. Carla Cassidy takes us back to CHEROKEE CORNERS in *Manhunt.* There's a serial killer on the loose, and only the heroine's visions can help catch him—but will she be in time to save the hero? *Against the Wall* is the next SPECIAL OPS title from Lyn Stone, a welcome addition to the line when she's not also writing for Harlequin Historicals. Finally, you knew her as Anne Avery, also in Harlequin Historicals, but now she's Anne Woodard, and in *Dead Aim* she proves she knows just what contemporary readers want.

Enjoy them all—and come back next month, when Silhouette Intimate Moments brings you even more of the best and most exciting romance reading around.

Yours,

Leslie J. Wainger
Executive Editor

Please address questions and book requests to:
Silhouette Reader Service
U.S.: 3010 Walden Ave., P.O. Box 1325, Buffalo, NY 14269
Canadian: P.O. Box 609, Fort Erie, Ont. L2A 5X3

Dead Aim
ANNE WOODARD

INTIMATE MOMENTS™

Published by Silhouette Books

America's Publisher of Contemporary Romance

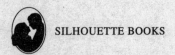 **SILHOUETTE BOOKS**

ISBN 0-373-27366-5

DEAD AIM

Books by Anne Woodard

Silhouette Intimate Moments

Dead Aim #1296

Other books written under the name Anne Avery

Harlequin Historicals

The Lawman Takes a Wife #573
The Bride's Revenge #618

ANNE WOODARD

After much wandering, Anne Woodard recently put down roots in Hawaii. With writing, cutting back a garden that won't stop growing and breaking up doggie squabbles because the Todd Man stole everyone's bones, she keeps busy. But not so busy that she can't explore the beauties of her new home state, including the local beaches! Readers can contact Anne at annewoodard1@earthlink.net.

Chapter 1

The sign swinging from the wrought-iron rack over the door said Cuppa Joe's in bright red letters. The painted placard propped in the window read, Coffee, Pastries, Homemade Sandwiches. Come On In!

The coffee shop was in the heart of the restored downtown of Fenton, Colorado, where a pedestrian mall had replaced the formerly traffic-choked street. The Victorian-style streetlamps were lit, making the fallen leaves glint amber and coppery red as they skittered across the mall in the cold autumn breeze. Light from the shop poured through the windows and into the street in a welcoming wash of gold.

But despite the inviting setting, the muscles in Rick Dornier's shoulders tensed.

His sister's college roommate, Grace Navarre, had sent him here. It seemed an unlikely place to find news of his missing sister, but he was running out of options.

Grace had been more interested in the joint she'd rolled than in Tina's disappearance. The last time she'd seen Tina, Grace had said Tina had been with some "hottie" at the Good Times bar. Grace seemed to think the existence of the hottie explained it all.

It didn't explain anything.

Serious, shy, hardworking Tina, whose only wild moment in her entire life, so far as he knew, had been moving in with someone like Grace, had been gone almost eight days before her roommate had mentioned the fact to a neighbor. Fortunately, the neighbor had had the good sense to notify the Grayson College police.

The campus cops had called his mother when they failed to turn up any trace of his sister. When even the local police drew a blank, his mother had put aside her own long-held resentments and called him.

Rick hadn't even stopped to unload his truck after his latest venture into the Montana backcountry. He told his boss he was taking whatever leave he'd accumulated, arranged for a colleague to cover his classes at the university, then driven all night to reach the small town of Fenton in the mountains west of Denver, which was home to Grayson College.

Tina was in her final year at the exclusive, private college. She expected to graduate summa cum laude next spring and had already been offered a full fellowship to pursue graduate studies in art history at Stanford University. From what he knew of her, the last thing she would have done is disappear for a week of wild sex with a stranger.

But then, he didn't know his own sister very well at all. Their parents, at war with each other since long before their divorce over eighteen years ago, had seen to that.

Although Rick had spent most of the day talking to the local police, the campus cops and all of Tina's professors he could find, he hadn't been able to find any leads. The few friends and classmates he'd been able to track down had been as casual as Grace about Tina's absence—college students were so accustomed to fellow students' irregular hours that they hadn't worried when they didn't see her around.

Tina had vanished without raising so much as a ripple in Grayson's small pond.

When Rick had pressed Grace for more information, all she would say was, "Ask Maggie."

She meant Maggie Mann, manager of the Cuppa Joe's, a woman, according to Grace, who knew everyone.

Rick just hoped she did. He was running out of options.

The inside of Cuppa Joe's was as funky as the name, an eclectic mix of chromed modern lights and solid turn-of-the-century oak tables and chairs that somehow fit well together. This early in the evening, about half of the tables were occupied, but any conversation was covered by the mellow jazz floating from hidden speakers. A college guy with a buzz cut and a T-shirt with the Grayson College logo on it was working the espresso machine with cheerful efficiency.

There was no sign of anyone named Maggie behind the counter.

"Can't decide?" The deep, feminine voice came from behind him.

Rick turned and blinked.

She wasn't beautiful, but she was the kind of woman that made a man's blood stir just to look at her—tall, slender, with full breasts, a narrow waist and long, shapely legs that fantasies were made of. Her hair was a casual tangle of short-cropped brown curls that made his fingers itch to touch them. Her nose would never grace *Vogue*'s cover. Her chin was too square, her mouth too wide and her eyes set too far apart under surprisingly dark, thick brows. And yet there was an appealing warmth in those dark eyes and an irresistible smile on that too-wide mouth that managed somehow to look just right on her face.

Rick swallowed, hard. "I'm sorry. Did you say something?"

"You have the look of a man in need of help," she teased.

"Are you Maggie?"

She nodded. "I'm Maggie. And you are…?"

"Rick." He cleared his throat. She had the oddest effect on him. "Richard Dornier."

"Rick Dornier?" A frown flitted across her face so quickly that he wasn't sure he'd really seen it. "Tina's brother?"

"You know Tina?"

"Sure. Almond latte. Decaf if it's after three. Cinnamon orange scone if we have them, or a slice of honey-bran nut bread if we don't." She laughed. He'd swear he heard bells ringing.

"She's such a sweetie," Maggie added, moving around to the back of the counter. "Where's she been? I haven't seen her for a couple weeks."

The casual comment made something catch in his chest. She was the first person who'd asked about his sister, the first person who'd noticed she hadn't been around.

He propped his elbows on the marble counter and leaned toward her. "I was hoping you could tell me where she is."

"Me?" The good humor vanished, and the light

in those dark green eyes sharpened. "Maybe you'd better explain."

"Tina's missing. She's been missing for almost two weeks, though her roommate didn't bother to notify anyone of that fact until a week ago. I'm trying to find her."

"Two weeks are a long time for someone like Tina to be gone." She studied him, not quite suspicious, but not nearly so friendly as she'd been a few moments before. "Have you talked to the police?"

"Yes. They checked around, but there was no trace of her, and no trace of…of problems."

He'd almost said foul play, and that shook him. He refused to consider that possibility. Not yet.

Maggie made a thoughtful little humming noise in her throat, then startled him by asking what he wanted to drink.

"What? Oh!" He straightened, disconcerted. "Uh…whatever. Coffee."

She plunked a thick white pottery mug down on the counter. "Plain old coffee's in those Thermoses over there. I'd suggest the dark roast—you look like you could use the caffeine. *And* some food. When's the last time you ate?"

"I— Look, coffee's fine, but I—"

"Can't help your sister if you keel over from hunger and exhaustion." She grabbed his hand and wrapped it around the mug. "And don't waste your time glaring at me like that. I'm immune."

Rick's finger obediently slipped through the handle of the mug before he had a chance to blink, let alone refuse.

"You go get your coffee," she added, opening the glass display case that contained a selection of pastries and plastic-wrapped sandwiches. "I'll grill you a ham and Brie sandwich and join you in a minute. Take the table in the corner by the window. It's quiet there and we can talk."

Rick opened his mouth to protest.

"Coffee and sandwich comes to six-fifty," she said briskly. And then she grinned and winked at him, and his protest turned into a laugh.

He tossed a ten-dollar bill on the counter and picked up the mug, still grinning. "You can bring the change with the sandwich."

As he settled at the corner table, Rick realized he felt better than he had all day. More hopeful, suddenly.

Thoughtfully, he rubbed the back of his hand. His skin still tingled where Maggie had touched him.

She was right—he wouldn't help Tina by forgetting to take care of himself. He'd spent enough time in the backcountry to know that the first guys to collapse on a grueling hike were always the ma-

cho fools who thought they were too tough to have
to stop for food, water and rest.

And the coffee really was good.

He had to force himself not to hitch his chair over
a foot or two so he could see around the potted
plant that blocked his view of Maggie Mann.

Rick Dornier wasn't anything like his delicate,
dark-haired sister, Maggie thought as she halved the
grilled sandwich, then set a couple of the spicy
Greek olives that were a specialty of Joe's beside
it.

Where Tina was pale from too many hours spent
studying, the brother was tall, sun-browned and quietly confident. Exactly the long, lean, broad-
shouldered kind of confident that she would have
expected of a man who made his living studying
grizzly bears in the wild. The day's growth of beard
shadowing his jaw simply added to the appeal.

Tina had told her about him. He was Dr. Dornier,
actually. A wildlife biologist who taught at some
university up in Montana, but who preferred to
spend his time in the wilderness studying his be-
loved bears.

What Maggie hadn't expected was the sudden,
intense…awareness that had struck her when he'd
turned that first time and she'd looked up into his
rugged, not-quite-handsome but undeniably appealing face.

She wasn't used to that. Over the years, her work had thrown her together with all sorts of men, and while some of them had been attractive, and a couple had become her lovers, not one had roused an instant reaction like this. She could still feel the lingering effects of the odd zing that had brought her senses to nerve-tingling attention, just at the sight of him.

Maybe *she* ought to have something to eat.

Instead, she gave herself a mental shake and fixed a cup of coffee for herself—it made people nervous when they were eating and drinking and you weren't. The last thing she wanted was for Rick Dornier to feel uncomfortable right now.

She picked up the plate with his sandwich. "I'm taking a break, Steve, okay?" she called to the young man who was expertly foaming milk for a cappuccino.

He nodded in acknowledgement but didn't take his attention off his masterwork.

Maggie grinned. It hadn't been that long ago she'd considered overbrewed sludge the standard for coffee and flavored artificial creamer the height of class. Her life was never going to be the same after Joe's.

As she always did, she paused to greet the customers she knew personally. An important part of her job was getting to know them, remembering names and faces and facts. Fortunately, it was also one of her favorite parts of the job.

She'd long ago accepted that the moral ambiguities involved were also part of the job, no matter how uncomfortable they sometimes were.

When she got to Rick's table, he surprised her by standing and pulling out a chair for her.

"Thanks."

"No, thank *you*. I hadn't realized how hungry I was 'til you brought up the subject." He slid into his chair with a distracting, loose-limbed grace, then took the plate from her and popped an olive into his mouth. "Mmmm. Good. The sandwich looks even better."

"It is." She let him take a couple of bites before she broached the question that interested her almost as much as it interested him. "Do you have any idea where Tina might be?"

He paused with the sandwich halfway to his mouth, then grimaced and set it back down.

"I was hoping *you* could tell me."

"Me? Why me?"

"Her roommate, Grace, suggested I talk to you. She said that Tina had mentioned you, talked about you."

"She did?" Maggie studied him warily. "Why would Tina talk about me?"

"I don't know. I guess she considered you a friend."

Maggie repressed a quick stab of guilt. She should be used to that by now, too. Guilt was another of those work-related ambiguities she had to live with.

"I liked Tina," she said, keeping her tone light. "We talked sometimes when I wasn't busy, or she wasn't lost in her studies. She never mentioned anything that might have kept her away from class for two weeks."

But was that because Tina had nothing to share, or because she didn't dare risk sharing it?

"You say the police looked into it?" She said it casually, careful to keep just the right note of concerned interest in her voice without playing it up too much.

"Yeah." He frowned at his scarcely eaten sandwich, then shoved the plate away. "They said there was nothing to indicate any problems, that a couple of people besides Grace mentioned a guy she was talking to at the Good Times bar. You know the place?"

Maggie nodded.

"Did Tina ever mention a man? A boyfriend? Somebody she might have gone away with for a couple of weeks?"

Maggie shook her head. "No. I got the impression she was more interested in her studies than in men."

"That's my impression, too. I know Mom

nagged her about it.'' He smiled a little wistfully. ''She looks like this quiet little mouse, but from what I've seen, she's got a mind of her own. Always thinking, though it isn't always easy to tell exactly *what* she's thinking.''

I noticed that, too. Maggie didn't express the thought to Rick.

''Were the police able to identify this guy Tina was seen talking to?'' she asked.

He shook his head. ''Grace said he looked sort of like Tom Cruise. A young Tom Cruise. Have you seen anyone like that around here?''

Maggie had to smile. ''This is a college town. It's swarming with good-looking, young guys, and more than a couple of them could give Tom Cruise a run for his money in the looks department.''

''I hadn't thought of that.''

''The police evidently did. Who'd you talk to down at the station?'' She made that question sound casual, too.

''An Officer Padilla. He wanted to be helpful, but…'' Rick shrugged, clearly frustrated. ''I talked to the chief of police, too.''

''You talked to David Bursey?'' She jerked upright in her chair, surprised.

''That's right.'' Dornier studied her. ''You know him?''

''A little,'' she said cautiously.

Damn! She would have to be a hell of a lot more

careful if Bursey was taking an interest in Tina's disappearance.

"He comes in every now and then for coffee," she said casually, as if it didn't matter. At least the part about the coffee was one hundred percent truthful. "What'd he say?"

His eyes narrowed angrily. "He said there was nothing to indicate a problem. That Tina had been seen talking to a good-looking guy, then evidently had gone home and packed a small bag and left. He said a lot of college kids did that when the opposite sex was more appealing than their studies."

"Not Tina." Maggie knew it, and if Bursey had taken the time to spin that little yarn for Tina's brother, then he knew it, too. The question was, how much else did the chief of police know? And what was she going to do about it?

"No," Dornier agreed grimly, "not Tina."

A sudden stab of…something—longing? Regret? Envy, maybe?—hit Maggie. What would it be like to have a brother who could get so quietly, dangerously angry at even a hint of doubt against you? Who would drop everything and drive eight hundred miles the minute he learned you were in trouble?

She forced the thought away. Life, she'd long ago decided, was what you made of whatever you were handed. Wishing for what you didn't have was a waste of energy.

"Have you talked to anybody besides the police?" she asked. "And Tina's roommate. What did you say her name was? Grace? Besides suggesting you talk to me, what did *she* say?"

Maggie had no intention of revealing just how much she knew about Grace Navarre. What she needed was to know how much Rick Dornier knew, then decide what she was going to do about it.

Even as Rick told Maggie about the people he'd talked to and the little information he'd gathered that day, he wasn't sure why he was doing it. He'd never been one to spill his guts to strangers...until now.

Maggie Mann made a good sandwich. She had a nice smile and a great body and just looking at her was distracting, but none of that was reason for chewing her ear off about his worries. Especially since she had more questions than he did, and not one answer. And yet, he couldn't stop talking. After twenty-four hours of nonstop worry, it was a relief to share that worry with someone who was as good a listener as Maggie.

"That's not much to go on," she admitted when he'd finished.

"No. But it's all I have right now." He glanced at his watch, then pushed his chair back from the table. "And I need to get moving if I'm going to learn any more. The Good Times bar was closed when I went by this afternoon, but they ought to be open by now. I'm hoping somebody there will know who the guy was that Tina was talking to the night she disappeared.''

Maggie was faster onto her feet. ''Finish your sandwich. I'll take you there. I know the people who work there and a lot of the regulars. But I have to call my boss first. Okay?''

He almost refused. Instead, after a moment's hesitation, he sank back in his chair.

''Thanks. Having you along really might help. I appreciate the offer.''

As she walked away, he found himself leaning forward so he could see around that damned potted plant. She had a graceful, long-legged stride that was real easy to watch, and she wore jeans like they'd been tailored just for her.

He'd always liked women and enjoyed being with them, but there was something about Maggie that stirred his blood in ways that weren't easy to ignore. And crazy as it seemed, just the thought of having her along made him feel a little more optimistic. He was used to hunting bears, not people, especially not people he cared for. At least Maggie knew Tina and the people at the bar. That was something, anyway.

After a brief word with the guy behind the counter, Maggie disappeared into the back room, and Rick settled back in his chair to wait.

Since he had nothing better to do, he pulled the now-cold cup of coffee to him, then picked up his sandwich. He started to take a bite, but something on the street outside caught his attention. The fine hairs at the back of his neck pricked, warning of danger.

He set the sandwich down and scanned the sidewalk in front of Joe's. Nothing there but strangers hurrying past, shoulders hunched against the wind and cold. He almost put it down to nerves and weariness and too much time spent in the wilderness looking for grizzlies when he spotted the man standing on the other side of the pedestrian mall.

Unlike the other passersby, the fellow seemed oblivious to the cold. He wore a down vest over a chambray work shirt and well-worn jeans. A Stetson pulled low obscured his features, but Rick recognized him easily.

What he couldn't figure was why the Fenton's chief of police should be standing out there in the dark and the cold, studying him like a hunter studying his prey.

Chapter 2

Her call was picked up on the first ring.

"It's me," Maggie said.

There was a pause at the other end of the line as her listener confirmed there were no bugs on the line, then a brusque, "Talk."

She shifted in the battered office chair to get a better view of the short hall outside the coffee shop's cramped office. Steve was busy behind the front counter, but Sharon Digby, the other employee due on tonight, had a useful habit of coming in early.

"Dornier's brother's here," she said, keeping her voice low.

That caught her listener's attention. "Her

brother? He was in Montana yesterday. We checked.''

''Yeah, well he's here now, and he's already been around town talking to people. His mother called him. He must have driven all night to get here.''

''Great. Just great.'' Another pause at the end of the line. ''Is he going to be a problem?''

The door from the shop opened. Maggie craned for a better look, then slid back a ways, out of sight. She waited until she heard the rest room door lock behind the customer before she spoke again.

''He hit the police station. Bursey spun him some story about college kids and hormones being more appealing than class work.''

''He talked to Bursey?''

''Bursey talked to him. Made a point of it.''

More silence while her listener digested that information. Then, ''You think he knows anything?''

''No.'' She thought about that, then added, ''Not yet. Playing cop isn't his thing, but he's smart and tough.''

''Guess you'd have to be if you chase grizzlies for a living.'' There wasn't any humor behind the words.

''He's worried about his sister.''

She fell silent at the sound of a toilet flushing, then water running. The rest room door opened, followed by footsteps heading back. The noise of conversation and the espresso machine working rose as the hall door opened, then dimmed as it swung shut. She craned to be sure the customer was gone, waiting for the confirming click of the latch as the door closed behind them.

"He's planning on visiting Good Times tonight," she said at last. "I'm going with him."

"All right. But keep a sharp eye on him. We can't afford to have any trouble at this point in the game."

Maggie frowned at the cluttered bulletin board on the wall above the desk, annoyed. "Anything else you want to tell me? Like how to tie my shoes or blow my nose?"

"Don't be so damned touchy. And yeah, there's something I want to tell you. Don't go off on your own. You're not a superhero."

She grinned. "Wanna bet?"

"Dammit!"

"You can say that again." This time, she wasn't smiling.

She set the receiver back in its cradle without bothering to say goodbye.

She knew exactly what he'd meant.

Dornier had his jacket on and was waiting near the counter when Maggie emerged. He looked a little tired, but Maggie would swear she sensed a tension in him that hadn't been there a few minutes

earlier. He didn't say anything, however, and she
didn't ask.

"Steve, I've gotta go," she said to the young
man behind the counter. "Sharon should be in
shortly. Think you can handle things until then?"

Steve grinned. "Sure. You know me."

Maggie blew him a teasing kiss. Her odd hours
and occasional, abrupt departures had raised a few
eyebrows at the beginning, but everyone was used
to them by now. She'd worked hard to make sure
they were.

She turned to Rick Dornier and found him studying her.

Again there was that odd jolt of intense awareness.

There was nothing rude or even particularly sexual in the way he looked at her, yet still it unsettled
her. It was one thing for him to be attracted to her—
that might prove useful. But the last thing she
needed now was to be as conscious of him as a
man as he was of her as a woman.

She forced the feeling down. She couldn't afford
to let anything distract her or throw her off balance.
Not right now.

Somehow, without even trying, Rick Dornier
managed to do both.

"Ready?" was all she said.

"Ready." Before she could stop him, he took her

jacket out of her hands and held it up so she could slip it on.

Maggie hesitated, then turned to allow him to help her, silently chiding herself for letting so simple a gesture catch her off guard like that. "Thanks."

"You're welcome."

She started to move away from him, but his hand on her shoulder stopped her.

"Hold on a second. Your collar's turned."

There wasn't anything remotely sexual about the way he flipped her collar over, then smoothed it into place, yet her body tensed involuntarily and the back of her neck burned where he touched her. She would swear she could still feel the heat of his hand where it had rested on her shoulder.

He flicked her unruly curls out from beneath her collar and stepped back. "There. That should do it."

She kept her head down and tugged up the zipper. Her throat felt tight and her breathing was fast and a little shallow, but she managed to keep her words light, teasing, in keeping with the Maggie everyone at Joe's thought they knew.

"Are all you Montana guys so well mannered?"

He laughed. The sound of it set her pulse racing.

"Blame it on my dad. He was hell on good manners."

He held the door for her, then automatically took

the street side of the sidewalk even if there weren't any cars to defend her from.

"My car's parked just around the corner," she said, forcing herself to look up at him.

She refused to admit that she was disappointed when she found he was scanning the street rather than looking at her.

"I'm a couple blocks farther down," he said. Yet when she turned the corner, he turned with her.

"You don't have to walk me to my car, you know." She couldn't quite suppress the irritation in her voice. "It's not that late, and Fenton isn't that dangerous."

"That's good. Which car's yours?"

"The red Subaru." She punched the automatic entry button on her key ring. The car beeped and unlocked the doors. The system was a safety mechanism, one she'd relied on more than once when she had to get away fast. Once, it had almost cost her her life.

He waited on the sidewalk while she walked around to the driver's side.

"I'll meet you at the bar, all right?" she said, silently willing him to go away *now* so she could get herself under control.

"Fine."

He was still standing there when she slid behind the wheel.

*   *   *

Maggie switched the key in the ignition. The Subaru's engine raced a little, then settled into a steady, comforting purr.

And he was *still* standing there.

Cursing herself for a fool, she leaned over and opened the passenger's side door.

"Get in. I'll drive you to your car."

It figured. The one man who had the power to addle her wits just by looking at her was also well mannered and annoyingly overprotective. And that was dangerously appealing, too. She would have to be extra careful. She didn't dare let herself get involved.

The Subaru was fairly roomy, but Rick Dornier took up a lot more space than she liked. She was finding it hard to breathe. The engine hadn't warmed enough to put out any heat, yet she would swear the temperature inside the car was rising.

By the time she dropped him off at his pickup a few minutes later, her chest was hurting from the effort to breathe. She made sure he knew how to get to the bar, but didn't wait for him even to unlock his door before her foot mashed down on the gas pedal.

Her tires squealed on the pavement as she roared away.

It was only the middle of the week, yet the parking lot at the Good Times bar was almost full when Rick arrived.

Maggie, shoulders hunched against the cold, was pacing in front of the door. He had the feeling she was regretting her offer to help, but before he could say a word, she yanked the door open and stepped inside. Frowning, Rick followed her.

Even in his college years, he hadn't been much for bars and partying. His friends ribbed him about his unsociable ways, but these days he generally stuck to the unfashionable places where he could get a beer and maybe engage in a little conversation about whatever game was showing on TV.

Walking into Good Times was like walking into a wall of heat and humanity. The bar was everything he hated—loud, crowded and trendy. A sign outside had advertised a live band for the weekend, but right now a popular country and western pop hit was blaring from hidden speakers that almost, but not quite, managed to cover the deafening roar of conversation and laughter.

The crowd was mostly college kids and young professionals, with an occasional aging, desperate male here and there trying to pretend that the years weren't catching up with him. Dress was everything from slick business suits to short tops, low jeans and navel rings. Judging from the expressions on their faces, all of these customers had one thing in common—a grim determination to have fun, no matter how much it hurt.

Rick tried to imagine Tina in a place like this and failed. Tina lived in the reverent quiet of libraries and museums, not this kind of insanity.

A tug on his sleeve drew his attention back to Maggie. He had to bend down to hear what she was shouting. She leaned closer, her breast touching his sleeve.

"I'm going to hit a friend at the bar, ask him about Tina, who all the regular patrons are, see if we can find someone who saw her. Order me a diet soda, will you?"

Her breath was warm on his ear. All he would have to do to kiss her was turn his head....

Before he could say a word, she'd handed him her jacket and slipped into the crowd, seemingly as comfortable in this madhouse as she was at the Cuppa Joe's. Just walking into the place had brought the sparkle back to her eyes.

Before Rick could follow her, a harried-looking waitress dodged in front of him with an overloaded tray of drinks. He edged around her and ran into three giggling females who eyed him with a speculative interest that drove him in the opposite direction. By the time he'd worked his way through the outer fringes of the crowd, he'd shucked his own jacket and lost Maggie completely.

Rick stared about him, baffled. He hadn't worked out any real plan, just figured he would talk to the bartenders and waitresses until he found someone who remembered Tina and the guy she'd been with. He hadn't counted on having to deal with a crowd like this or noise levels that made it impossible to talk below a shout.

He wished Maggie were beside him. She seemed to be at home in a place like this.

He would swear he could still catch her lingering scent on his jacket sleeve where she'd inadvertently pressed against him.

Too much time in the wilderness, Dornier, he chided himself, ruthlessly squelching the thought.

Because Maggie was already talking to the people tending bar, and because Rick couldn't think of anything else to do, he stopped the next waitress and asked if she knew a Tina Dornier. She looked at him as if he'd lost his mind.

"It's all I can do to remember the drink orders." She glanced at his empty hands. "You want one?"

He didn't. It was only after she was gone that he remembered he was supposed to order Maggie a diet soda.

He scanned the crowd, struggling against dismay. What in hell had he been thinking? He dealt with grizzlies, not humans engaged in modern courtship rituals. Maggie had been right—there were a lot of good-looking guys here, any number of whom could have given Tom Cruise a run for his money.

The last thing people at a place like this would pay attention to was a quiet woman talking to a man nobody knew.

Was there something else he could do to find out the name of that stranger Tina had been talking to the last time anyone had seen her?

Or, at least, admitted to having seen her.

That thought made him flinch.

As it turned out, the people came to him. The women, anyway, many of them younger than Tina. Several offered to buy him a drink. Not one remembered his sister, let alone the stranger.

Desperate, he grabbed a small table that was just opening up. He draped Maggie's jacket over the back of the second chair, then stopped another passing waitress and ordered a beer and diet soda.

She was back sooner than he'd expected.

"Tina?" she said in answer to his query. She set the soda on the table. "Sure, I know her."

She handed Rick the beer, deftly pocketed the twenty he handed her, then brightened when he refused any change. Thus encouraged, she set down her tray and slid into the empty seat across from him.

"Tina's two years ahead of me, but she helps me and a couple of friends with art history papers sometimes. Real nice. And she's your sister?" She eyed him assessingly.

Rick found himself blushing. "She was in here

a couple weeks ago. Talking to some stranger, according to her roommate.''

The girl frowned. ''I remember Tina being here. Good Times isn't, like, exactly the sort of place she hung out. Know what I mean? But a guy…?''

She scanned the crowd as if hoping for inspiration. ''I sorta remember seeing her with someone, because Tina wasn't really interested in guys. You know? I remember he was good-looking, but there's, like, *lots* of good-looking guys here.''

''Her roommate said he looked like Tom Cruise,'' Rick offered helpfully.

''Tom Cruise?'' She frowned, considering, then shrugged. ''I don't know. We don't get many guys that old in here, you know?''

Rick managed not to laugh.

Karin stood. ''I'd better get going or my boss'll dock my pay or something. You got a number I can call if I think of anything?''

''Not yet. I haven't had time to get a hotel room. But here's my business card.''

''What about your cell phone?''

''I don't have a cell phone.''

She stared at him as if he'd suddenly grown two heads.

It was a look Rick had seen before. His friends thought he was a Neanderthal, but he'd never understood the modern passion for instant communication. Besides, cell phones weren't all that useful

in Montana's backcountry—too many places where
you couldn't get a signal. "Can I leave a message
for you here?" was all he said. "To let you know
where you can reach me if you remember anything?"

"Sure. There's always someone here who can
take a message if I'm not working. My name's
Karin. With an 'i.'"

"Thanks, Karin." He smiled. "I'll remember the
'i.'"

A couple of minutes later, Maggie slid into the
chair Karin had vacated. She snatched up the soda
and took a couple big gulps.

"Thanks! Trying to carry on a conversation in
this place is hard work."

Like Karin, she had to lean halfway across the
table and shout to make herself heard over the
noise. You could plot a bank robbery here and the
folks at the next table wouldn't hear a word you'd
said.

"Find out anything?"

She shook her head. The movement made a stray
curl on her forehead bounce. "How about you?"

Rick repressed an urge to brush the curl into
place.

"Nothing. One person who knows Tina and re-
members seeing her here, but that's it."

He had to fight not to shove his chair back and

put as much distance between him and Maggie as he could.

He hadn't thought twice about getting close enough to Karin so they could talk, but, then, she hadn't made his pulse rate soar just by looking at her.

"It would be easier if I had a better description of the man she was talking to," he said.

"Yeah. I tried that 'Tom Cruise look-alike' line on one of the bartenders."

"And…?"

"He laughed at me."

Rick stared at her, unsmiling. She stared right back, quietly assessing.

"I'm running out of options here," he grimly admitted, more to himself than to her.

She considered that, then shook her head. "Not quite. Let's go talk to Grace, again."

Maggie stood abruptly, reaching for her jacket. "Come on. We might get lucky and catch her at home."

"I didn't get the impression Grace was all that serious about her studies."

There wasn't any humor in the look Maggie gave him.

"I didn't say anything about interrupting her studying."

Rick followed Maggie as she worked her way through the crowd. He was going on two days without sleep, and the noise of Good Times had given him a headache, but he didn't even consider finding a hotel. Not yet. There wasn't much hope they would get anything useful out of Grace—even if they found her home, which he doubted. She was probably so stoned by now that she didn't even remember who Tina was—but he couldn't think of anything else to do, and he had to do *something*.

They were almost to the door when Maggie stopped in her tracks.

Rick placed his hand at the small of her back in an instinctive, almost protective gesture. He could feel the tension in her body even through the thickness of her jacket.

Standing just inside the entrance, watching them, was Fenton chief of police, David Bursey.

Maggie moved forward, deliberately casual. "Chief Bursey."

Bursey touched the brim of his Stetson politely. "Ms. Mann."

"Your hat's still on. Are you coming in or going out?"

"Guess that depends."

Maggie ignored that barb. "I don't recall seeing you here before."

His gaze flicked from Maggie to Rick and back again. "Rumor has it you're here quite a bit."

Maggie's chin came up. "That's right. Even a

coffeehouse waitress likes a little action now and then. Anything wrong with that?''

"Not usually, no.''

Bursey's tone was casual, bland, even, yet Rick heard the warning beneath the surface. But what was Bursey warning them against?

He shifted to let a patron get past him. The rush of air from the open door was cold and clean, welcome after the stale air of the bar. He caught a glimpse of a man in the doorway, head lowered, his shoulder raised as he awkwardly shrugged into his coat. Then the man was gone and the outer door swung shut.

Beside him, Maggie settled her own jacket more comfortably on her shoulders. "See you around, Dave.''

It was a challenge, not a question.

The police chief nodded. "Sure, Maggie. You know what I think of you and the Cuppa Joe's.''

"Yeah,'' said Maggie coolly. "I know.''

"And you, Dr. Dornier,'' the chief added, shifting his attention to Rick. Beneath the broad brim of the Stetson, the man's eyes narrowed. "You hear anything about your sister, you let us know.''

Rick held that hard gaze for a minute, fighting down anger. What in hell was all this about? More important, what did it have to do with Tina?

"Yeah,'' he said. "I'll do that.'' He turned to Maggie. "Ready?''

She was out the door before he could open it for her, her car keys in her hand. Swearing, Rick pulled on his own coat and started after her.

From the far side of the lot came the sound of an engine starting. It wasn't enough to drown the voice from the doorway behind him.

"Mr. Dornier? Rick? Rick! Wait up!"

It was the waitress, Karin. She hadn't even bothered to grab a coat before rushing outside. From the corner of his eye, Rick saw Maggie stop, then walk back toward them, but he wasn't concerned about her right now.

Karin came to a panting halt beside him. "That man you were looking for? The one Tina was talking to? I saw him!"

He stiffened, the cold and Bursey both forgotten. "What? Where? He's inside?"

She shook her head, then wrapped her arms around her body, shivering. "I'm not *real* sure, you know? But I'm *pretty* sure it's him. I noticed him because he's *really* good-looking? And then I noticed that he was watching you and Maggie and I thought, Wow! That's him!"

Rick gritted his teeth against the urge to shake her. "Where is he now?"

Karin was almost dancing from cold and excitement. "He left. Right before you did. He walked right by you. I thought sure you'd see him!"

At the far side of the lot, a black Ford pickup

pulled out of its space. The driver, invisible at this distance, pulled into the street without stopping and sped away.

Maggie was already running. Rick caught the beep of the electric door locks on her car.

"Come on!" she shouted. "My car's closest!"

He barely managed to squeeze into the passenger seat and slam the door shut before she roared out of the parking lot after the pickup.

Chapter 3

The pickup was three blocks away and moving fast.

The speed limit was thirty-five. Maggie was doing fifty by the time she'd reduced the gap to a block and a half. Ahead, the traffic light changed from green to amber.

Her grip on the wheel tightened as she scanned the intersection. She slowed just enough to confirm there were no cars coming, then roared on through as the light changed from amber to red.

Thank God it was the middle of the week and most people were home rather than out partying.

Maggie glanced in her rearview mirror—no cops in sight—then stepped on the gas. When there were

only two cars remaining between them and the
pickup, she slowed, then dodged behind a minivan.

Beside her, Rick Dornier strained forward, heed-
less of the seat belt cutting him in half. ''You can
catch him if you step on it.''

The whiplash urgency of his words told her all
she needed to know about his fears for his sister's
safety. Fears he probably hadn't admitted, even to
himself.

''We want to follow him, not scare him off,'' she
said. But the next chance she got, she zoomed past
the minivan, hoping their quarry wouldn't notice.

Now there was only one car between them.

She easily made it through two more stoplights,
but had to push it to slip through the third. And
then there weren't any lights at all for a while. Traffic was steady, but too light. The longer they were
behind the pickup, the greater the chances its driver
would spot them.

Worried, Maggie dropped back and let another
car slide in front of her.

''That guy's gotta know he's being followed.''
Rick words came out calm, controlled, but Maggie
could hear the tension underlying them.

''Doesn't matter,'' Maggie lied. Out of the corner of her eye she saw him glance at her, his gaze
sharp, assessing. If her wild driving bothered him,
he hadn't given any sign of it.

''What matters is we don't lose him,'' she

amended, braking slightly to let another car slide in between her and the pickup, now three cars up.

"What matters is that I want to talk to him." Rick's gaze was still fixed on her, a fact that Maggie, who prided herself on her imperviousness, was finding oddly unsettling.

His eyes seemed to glow gold in the darkness of the car's interior. Like a wolf's, she thought, then forced her attention back to the road.

She knew the instant he looked away—it was as if he'd suddenly let go of the invisible cord on which he'd held her.

Ahead, the driver of the pickup slowed and abruptly turned left, without signaling. There wasn't room to pass the car ahead before the turn, but the instant Maggie got the Subaru's nose into the turn, the pickup was already at the next intersection and accelerating fast.

"You might want to step on it," Rick suggested in a voice whose calmness couldn't quite mask the dangerous tension beneath the surface. "If he didn't know he was being followed before, he does now."

Maggie shot him an annoyed glance and stepped on it.

"He's turning! There! Down that alley." Rick smacked the dashboard in frustration. "He's spotted us, dammit!"

"Yeah, but that doesn't mean he's going to ditch us."

Maggie whipped the Subaru into the alley. The sturdy little car bucked as it hit a pothole, then another. The headlights carved a mad slash against the unlit blackness, highlighting a battered Dumpster, some abandoned crates and the faceless brick walls of the buildings on either side.

At the other end of the alley, the driver of the pickup shot across the next street and back into the unlit alley beyond. The driver of the car he'd almost rammed laid on the horn in protest. The angry wail grew louder as Maggie shot across the street, then faded again as she drove into the alley after the truck.

Beside her, Rick cursed as she hit another pothole and his head hit the roof.

They burst out of the alley and into a tire-squealing turn as the pickup turned left and roared the wrong way up the one-way street.

He didn't try that stunt again, but Maggie almost lost him more than once as he wove his way through the traffic and the warren of alleys and one-way streets that marked this part of town.

Eventually, he gave up trying to shake them and turned onto an old two-lane highway leading out of town.

"Where does this road go?" Rick was leaning forward, hands braced against the dashboard, his attention fixed on the truck ahead of them like a hungry wolf hot on the scent of his prey.

In the cramped confines of the car, he seemed a lot bigger than he had in the coffee shop, leaner and more dangerous.

"North," she said. "Into the mountains."

"Where all he needs to do to ditch you is find a really bad four-wheel-drive road."

Maggie couldn't stop the growl of disgust that rose in her throat. "Yeah. And around here, we've got plenty of those."

Ahead, the truck speeded up to pass a car, then another truck. He slid back into his lane just before an oncoming car prevented Maggie from following him. Then taillights flared as the pickup's driver braked suddenly, then turned off the highway and headed toward the mountains.

"I think you mentioned something about four-wheel-drive roads?" The Subaru bucked and bounced as Maggie followed the truck off the paved road and onto a rough, rocky dirt road.

The car's shocks would never be the same. She figured they covered a couple miles of bone-jarring rough road before the pickup turned again and disappeared in the tangle of trees and shrubs that lined the road. Gravel spattered from under her tires as she stomped on the brakes, bringing the car to a juddering stop.

In the headlights' glare, the rocky trail the pickup had taken looked like an impassable river of jagged rock that slashed through the trees to disappear in the dark beyond. Nothing short of a four-wheel-drive vehicle would make it up that road, and Maggie wasn't sure she would attempt it even then.

Rick drew in a deep, slow breath, then let it out, obviously fighting for control. His eyes were like black holes in his rough-hewn face, unreadable and dangerous. For a college professor, he was a lot tougher than she'd expected.

A professor who studied grizzlies, she reminded herself, and wondered again at the difference between brother and sister.

"It'll be easy enough to find him tomorrow," he said. "There can't be much up there. A cabin, maybe."

"Or nothing at all," Maggie said bleakly. "He may have headed up there knowing we couldn't follow him…and that there was nothing to find up there to find when we did."

She studied the trail the pickup had taken, her thoughts racing.

Why had Tina disappeared? No mere art student, certainly not one as devoted to her studies as Tina, just up and left in the middle of the semester. And who was the man who'd just vanished up this rocky trail where they couldn't follow him? And why had he done it? He had to be involved in all this. She didn't know how, but she was absolutely sure he was. Innocent bystanders didn't lead others on wild car chases or duck onto a mountain trail like this in the middle of the night.

It took a moment for her to realize that Dornier was staring at her, his gaze boring into her with disconcerting force.

Maggie put the Subaru back into gear, suddenly uncomfortable under his assessing stare. "Might as well head back. I don't intend to sit around here, waiting for him to come back down."

"Give me a minute." He was out of the car before she could respond.

Frowning, she set the brake, turned off the engine, then got out of the car, too. By the time she reached his side, he'd already piled four or five good-sized stones in a little cairn at the edge of the track.

"You're coming back."

He set another rock on the pile, then nodded. "First thing in the morning."

"I'm coming with you." This was the first break they'd had in weeks. She had to know who'd been driving that pickup, and why, and where he'd been going, and Rick Dornier was going to help her find the answers whether he liked it or not.

Rick straightened, hesitated, then said, "All right."

"You'll have to drive, though."

He didn't say anything, just stood there staring at her, his expression unreadable in the dark.

Maggie deliberately stared right back. "What?"

"Most coffee shop managers I know don't drive like they were trying for the Indy 500."

So much for being helpful. Or hoping he wouldn't think to wonder.

"My mama always did say I got into the wrong business," she said lightly. "I never quite got over the fact they wouldn't buy me a dirt bike when I was eight, like I wanted."

"I could see where that might irritate you." He didn't sound convinced.

Maggie bent and grabbed a rock at random, then dumped it on the small pile he'd built. "That should be good enough."

She deliberately didn't look at him as she dusted off her hands, then walked back to the driver's side door.

"You coming?" she demanded, yanking open the door. "Or do you want to camp out here in the wilderness, waiting for whoever it is to come back down?" She slid behind the wheel, then stuck her head back out. "Might be a long, cold wait."

She was almost sorry when he slid in beside her. He really did fill up the car more than she was used to.

"Home, James," she said lightly. She didn't even wait for him to buckle his seat belt before she swung the car around, then set off, more sedately this time, on the road back to town.

* * *

Anger bubbled in Rick, and fear, though he wasn't yet willing to admit to the fear. An innocent man didn't run from following cars. Not the way this fellow had.

Whatever Tina had gotten herself into, it wasn't just a wild fling with a good-looking guy.

Because he couldn't bear to follow that thought, he focused on the landmarks that reared up in the headlights alongside the road, then disappeared in the dark behind. A crooked mailbox here, a gated driveway there. It would all look different in the daylight, but he would recognize them, anyway, and know just how far he would have to go to find that little rock cairn he'd built. First thing tomorrow, he promised himself grimly. He prayed that there was something up there that would lead him to Tina and not be just a dead end where that pickup's driver had gone to ground, waiting in safety until he could come back down and disappear, taking with him their only good link to finding Tina.

Only once they were back on the paved road did he stop watching for markers and focus on the silent woman beside him.

She was relaxed now, loose, only one hand on the wheel, but she was still pushing the speed limit, alert and confident. He had the feeling that she saw everything and everyone they passed, catalogued it, filed it away for future reference. Just as he did when he was in the backcountry, hunting for any sign of bear and what they'd been up to. She was city, he was country, but under the skin, they were a lot alike.

He wasn't sure he much liked the thought.

He wasn't sure he trusted her, either. Maggie Mann was not just a friendly, helpful coffee shop manager. Underneath that helpful persona she wore with such grace, there was an edge to her, an alertness, that reminded him of a couple of top-flight cops he knew.

And just what did that mean for Tina? Was Tina involved in something…illegal?

The thought shook him even as he ruthlessly shoved it aside.

Impossible. He might not know his sister as well as he would like—their mother had seen to that—but he did know that Tina was a strictly law-abiding, straight-and-narrow type of person. An art history major, not a drug dealer or thief or whatever else Maggie Mann might suspect. He was sure of it.

Rick shifted so he could get a better look at the woman in the seat beside him. She didn't move, didn't take her eyes off the road in front of them, but he would swear she tensed.

She didn't like him studying her.

Good. If she was after Tina, he wanted her off balance, uncertain.

In the light from the instrument panel her face seemed more finely drawn, more delicate, yet dangerous, too. Cop or not, he had to admit that she was a woman you noticed. Not pretty, but unforgettable. Not safe, but then, for him, danger had always had its own appeal.

In other circumstances, he would have asked her out, maybe angled to get her into bed. Too bad these weren't other circumstances.

Tina was missing and for some reason, Maggie Mann wanted to know why almost as much as he did. But not because she gave a damn about Tina.

Rick shifted in his seat, sliding his left arm along the back of her seat.

"So," he said, as casually as if he planned to chat about the weather. "What are you? A cop?"

That brought her head around with a snap. "What?"

"I figure you're undercover, right? Have to be. College town. College kids. Drugs have to be a problem, right?"

"I'm not a cop."

"DEA, then."

She glanced at him, then back at the road. The collar of her jacket brushed against his hand where it rested on the seat back. The nylon shell was cool to the touch, but he'd swear he could feel the heat of her beneath it.

"You're crazy."

"I've been accused of that a time or two," he admitted. "But I've never been accused of being stupid. That driving earlier? You were trained. Had to be."

"I told you—"

"Yeah. You're still angry that you didn't get a dirt bike when you were a kid. Maybe. I can believe the bit about the dirt bike. But you followed that guy like a real pro. That kind of driving doesn't happen just because someone fancies the idea of a little Motocross. You were trained to tail a car, trained for a high-speed chase."

She shrugged. She tried to make it look like an expression of irritation, maybe anger, but she couldn't quite pull it off. Underneath the irritation, she was wary as a cat.

"You've never heard of trying to help a friend?"

"I've heard of it."

"Ever heard of being grateful?"

The cat had claws. Sharp ones.

"Look, I don't give a damn if you're a cop or not. But I do give a damn about my sister. You didn't plunge into that chase just because you wanted to help. You wanted to know who that guy was and where he was headed as much as I did. Maybe more. I think I have a right to know why."

The look she shot him was pointed enough to draw blood.

''You have *no* rights, and there's nothing that says I have to put up with this. Or haul you back to town, for that matter.''

She had both hands clamped on the wheel now. He could see her curling and uncurling her fingers, probably fighting against the urge to let go of the wheel and wrap them around his throat.

Instead, she lifted her chin up and shoved her shoulders back. The thick curls at the back of her head brushed against the top of his hand, silken and cool. The inadvertent touch sent fire licking across the back of his hand.

An image flashed through his mind—of him grabbing those curls and pulling her head back. Of her throat curving, suddenly vulnerable, and her mouth opening.

Of him, kissing her.

The image was so immediate and vivid that he sucked in his breath, startled.

Sometimes there was a thin line between the adrenaline rush of anger and the equally hot, dangerous rush of sex. He'd seen it in the wild, but he'd never experienced it himself. Until now.

He didn't much like it.

He pulled his arm off the back of her seat. The car was too small and she was way too close.

Tina. Think of *Tina.*

The thought brought him back to his senses as effectively as if he'd been dunked in an ice-crusted mountain lake.

Where in the name of all that was holy was she?

They were in town, now, almost to the edge of downtown. A digital clock on a bank flashed the hour. It was later than he'd thought.

He was tired, Rick realized suddenly. Bone tired. He hadn't slept for two days, not since his mother had broken the news of Tina's disappearance. Was that really only yesterday?

He slumped back, let his head tilt back, his eyes close. One deep breath. Two. He drew the air in deep, forcing his chest to expand to take it all in, then slowly breathed out.

It helped. Not much, but it did help.

He forced himself to sit up.

"I have to stop at the shop," Maggie said abruptly, shattering the silence. "Make sure they're okay closing up. I'll take you to your truck as soon as I've checked in."

"That's all right. I'll get a cab."

"Fine."

Rick winced at the angry edge in her voice, then wearily dragged his hand across his face. The rasp of stubble reminded him he hadn't bothered to shave this morning. Hadn't even bothered to change clothes.

He probably looked like something Maggie

should have tossed out of her coffee shop two seconds after he'd walked in. Instead, she'd done her best to help him. Whatever her reasons, she didn't deserve the rude distrust he'd just dished out.

"I owe you an apology, Ms. Mann," he said. "A big one. I was out of line."

That jolted Maggie out of her thoughts. She glanced at him, surprised.

"*Way* out of line," she agreed dryly.

It was weariness that put the roughness in his voice, she realized. Weariness and worry. If she'd been in his place, looking for a sister who'd been missing for over two weeks, she would have been a whole lot more obnoxious.

She would like to think she would have been as good at putting two and two together and coming up with five as Rick Dornier, but she wouldn't like to bet on it.

Whether he really believed what he'd said or not, Rick had nailed her. The question was, what was she going to do about it?

Nothing, she decided. For now.

Still, if her boss found out that Rick had pegged her as undercover DEA within hours of meeting her, Garrity would pull her off the job. She couldn't let that happen. She was too close to finding out who was behind the sudden influx of high-quality Asian White heroin that was flowing into Colorado and the neighboring states to let anyone stop her now.

Her instincts told her Tina was involved in it somehow. Probably not as a dealer, but she knew something. Maggie was sure of it. But what? And why had she disappeared?

Or been made to disappear?

The thought made Maggie shiver.

Whatever Tina was up to, she was at risk. The sooner they found her, the better.

If she'd found Greg sooner—

Angrily, Maggie shoved the thought aside.

She liked Tina. A lot. But she couldn't afford to let her liking a person get in the way of doing her job. And she wouldn't let her own emotions get in the way of working with a man who might prove useful.

One thing, she was *not* going to let him get under her skin like he had. This was business, not personal. She needed to remember that.

Maggie relaxed her grip on the wheel, forced herself to relax.

"Apology accepted," she said lightly. "Actually, I suppose I should be flattered. No one's ever accused me of being a DEA agent before."

Not while she was undercover, anyway.

"And you won't need to call a cab," she added. "This time of night, it can take forever to get one. I won't be five minutes, tops."

* * *

Five minutes turned into thirty. There'd been a rush in the last hour so Steve and Sharon were tired and running very late.

To Maggie's surprise, Rick pitched in to help clean up. The man was clearly exhausted, but too darned nice to sit when others were overworked and eager to get home.

Maggie tucked the evening's take into the small office safe, shoved the stack of paperwork she'd meant to get to tonight to one side—working undercover like this meant she ended up doing two jobs, not one—and locked the office behind her. Dora, the morning manager, would have too much to do getting the shop ready to open at six to worry about whatever Maggie had left undone.

She emerged to find Sharon shrugging into her coat while Steve turned out the lights. Rick was standing in the middle of the room, hands in his pockets, wearily staring at nothing.

Maggie squelched a sudden urge to wrap her arms around him and tell him not to worry, that it was all going to work out somehow.

Helping Rick Dornier was part of her job, she sternly reminded herself. She wanted to find Tina and so did he. It was as simple as that. She was *not* getting emotionally involved here.

The sound of her footsteps on the old wood floor evidently roused him from his thoughts, for he blinked and gave himself a little shake. And then he smiled at her, a tired, intimate little smile that made something tighten in her chest.

She saved her smile for the two college kids. "Thanks, guys. I sure appreciate your staying late to finish up. I'll lock up behind you."

"We've still gotta take out the trash," Sharon protested, pointing to two well-filled plastic bags that had been set by the back door.

"I'm parked out back," Maggie assured her. "I'll get them. You two go on home. See you to-morrow."

The click of the lock as she closed the door behind them sounded unusually loud. She paused a moment in the entry. To make sure her employees were all right, she told herself. Her hesitation had nothing to do with the man still in the shop, waiting for her.

At this hour of the night, the pedestrian mall was quiet, the restaurants and upscale bars the only places still open, and even they would be closing soon. She flicked off the lights, plunging the shop into shadow. Behind her, Rick Dornier stirred. "That's it?"

"That's it." Maggie jiggled the doorknob to make sure. The low-wattage security light over the bar and the dull-gold light slipping in from the streetlights outside only made the shadows seem darker and bigger.

Rick Dornier loomed in the darkness, solid, human, inescapably male. Maggie's nerve endings pricked into life.

"I'm sorry it took so long. We don't usually get so many customers so late on a weeknight."

"No problem."

The only illumination in the back hallway was the emergency exit sign, but Maggie didn't need to look to know where he was. She could *feel* him there, right behind her, close enough to touch if she wanted.

Instead, she opened the back door, then grabbed the overstuffed trash bags Sharon had left there. "Get the locks, will you?"

The cold night air hit her like a slap in the face.

The man who lunged out of the inky shadows by the door was swinging something that would do a lot more damage when it landed.

Chapter 4

Instinct saved her.

Maggie ducked, then pivoted, swinging the only weapons immediately available—the trash bags she held in each hand.

The first hit and bounced off.

Her attacker, already off balance with the momentum of his swing, tried to dodge. The move made him stagger, then fall to one knee. Before he had a chance to realize what had hit him, she clobbered him with the second bag.

That one was heavier. Instead of bouncing off, it ripped, showering him in wet coffee grounds, sopping paper towels and napkins and the mushed remains of uneaten food.

Maggie had already released the first bag. When she let go of the second, it still contained enough trash that it plopped on the ground in front of him rather than flying off into the shadows.

Her attacker cursed, surged to his feet and stepped squarely in the slippery mess. His feet were already sliding out from under him when she swung back around and kicked him in the rear.

"Maggie! Behind you!"

Rick's shouted warning made her duck and roll just as something long and heavy hissed down, slicing through the space she'd occupied an instant before. She completed her roll and was on her feet before the second attacker could recover.

Behind her, she caught the wet sound that a fist made when it connected, hard, with bare flesh and soft bone. Out of the corner of her eye she saw the man try to recover from the first hit, then stagger as Rick landed a second, harder blow to the jaw.

She didn't have time to spare another glance—the first man had recovered his balance and was coming after her again.

She ducked, feinted right, then spun left, but not fast enough. The weighted pipe he was swinging caught her on the left shoulder.

It was a glancing blow, but it hit with enough force to draw a grunt of pain and send her to knees.

He'd expected her to roll away. Instead, she lunged toward him, low and fast. The heel of her hand connected where she'd aimed—right on his kneecap, where the force of the blow should at least knock him down if it didn't cripple him outright.

She felt bone crunch on impact.

Cripple him, then. Good. That helped.

She rolled away, got to her feet, then spun and kicked with all her might.

She'd been aiming for his other knee, but this guy was a bully, not a trained fighter. Instead of preparing to counter her next blow, he was folding in on himself, reaching for his injured knee.

Her foot connected with his ribs. It wasn't a well-placed blow, and she was still too off balance to put a lot of force behind it, but it was enough. He let out his breath in an explosive gasp of pain and dropped, then rolled away, out of reach.

Maggie turned, ready to help Rick, only to find he'd flattened his opponent and was already shoving the guy onto his face. The hold Rick had on the fellow's arm, which he'd twisted up behind his back, assured a groaning compliance.

"You all right?" Rick demanded. The raw fury in his voice startled her.

"Fine."

More or less.

She forced herself to straighten. Now that the adrenaline was beginning to seep away, her shoulder was starting to throb. Gingerly, she lifted her arm.

Rick was on his feet faster than she would have thought possible for a man his size.

"*Not* fine. Your shoulder—" He gently took her elbow. "You're hurt."

"Just a little," she admitted. The concern in his voice shook her more than the injury.

Cautiously, she swung her arm back, up, to the side, testing its limits. "It's a bruise. Nothing's broken."

"You don't know—"

"I know." She shrugged out of his grip. "I'm fine."

"You're crazy."

"And you're not even breathing hard," she snapped. Her heart felt like it was pounding against the inside of her rib cage.

"That's because I was too damn scared to breathe at all."

She couldn't help but laugh.

She glanced at the fellow spread-eagled, face-down on the ground at their feet. In the dark of the alley, the pulped, discarded napkins and half-eaten food that had spilled out of the ruptured garbage bag dotted the pavement, pale mush against the black.

"Oh, man…" Her voice trailed off in disgust. "Look at all this garbage I'm going to have to clean up!"

"He shouldn't be that much trouble," Rick assured her, straight-faced. "Even if he isn't very happy about the state of his nose right now."

From the corner of her eye, Maggie caught a movement in the shadows.

In an instant, the gun she hadn't had a chance to draw earlier was out of her pocket and in her hands.

"Freeze or I'll shoot!"

The second man, who'd been trying to crawl away, froze as ordered, then slowly, unhappily, stretched out, face-down on the ground, and laced his hands behind his head.

Silently cursing at her blown cover, Maggie shifted her grip on the gun, then drew her cell phone from her other pocket and handed it to Rick. "You want to call 9-1-1?"

She couldn't help but notice that he wasn't smiling as he dialed.

The clock on the police station wall said it was twenty-seven minutes past twelve. Rick's body told him it was a good twenty-four hours past his bedtime.

Any other time, he would have found an out-of-the-way corner, rolled his coat into a pillow and stretched out for a nap. He'd slept on enough rocky ground over the years that a hard floor was no impediment to sleep, especially not when he was as tired as he was now.

What he wanted right now, however, wasn't sleep. He wanted answers.

Answers that were in extremely short supply.

There'd been plenty of questions. Questions from the officers who'd responded to the 9-1-1 call. Questions from the sergeant on duty in the station. And then more questions from two irritable plainclothes types who didn't know whether to be more annoyed by what might be a premeditated attack on one of their own, or by being dragged out of bed in the middle of the night for what might simply be an attempted burglary gone bad.

When he'd finally lost his temper and demanded to know what in the hell all this had to do with his sister's disappearance, he'd been handed another cup of bad coffee and relegated to the plastic visitors' chairs in the hall. He would have called a cab long ago, but Maggie was still in that room down the hall on the right, talking to the two plainclothes and to Chief David Bursey, who hadn't been in any too good a mood, either.

Rick sipped his coffee and listened to the muffled sound of voices raised in anger coming from behind that door on the right.

Maggie had answers. He wasn't leaving her alone until he had them, too.

The door on the right opened. Maggie was the first out, furious and moving fast. An angry protest came from the room behind her, but she didn't stop and she didn't look back.

Rick set his coffee cup on a low table littered with other abandoned cups and got to his feet.

Maggie sailed past him without so much as a glance. "Ready?"

"Ready."

She was already halfway to the outer door.

"Manion!"

The angry shout from the hall behind them brought her to a halt, one hand on the push bar for the door. For an instant, Rick thought she was simply going to walk on out. Instead, she turned, head high, shoulders defiantly squared.

"Yeah?"

David Bursey halted at the opposite end of the room, hands fisted on hips, head lowered like a bull about to charge. Behind him, the two plainclothes men watched and waited.

"Don't think you can go haring off on your own, dammit! You worked for me, I'd bust your butt."

Maggie's chin came up. "I don't work for you anymore, remember?"

"You're too emotionally involved in this, Manion," Bursey growled. "I know it. You know it. You get involved, you make mistakes. And in this business, mistakes can cost lives."

Maggie's chin came up another inch. "I'm not

dropping this, Bursey. And I'm not making a mistake.''

And then she spun back around and marched out of the building. She moved so fast, the door had almost closed by the time Rick slipped out behind her.

Maggie beeped the car doors open but didn't bother to look to see if Rick was following. She slid behind the wheel, then simply sat there, the keys in her hand, blankly staring out the windshield. Her thoughts were such an angry jumble that she couldn't grab hold of anything, couldn't think what she ought to do next.

Rick slid in beside her, then slammed the door so hard it made her jump.

"The key goes in the ignition," he said. "Then you fasten your seat belt, turn on the engine and drive away. Think you can do that?"

His anger cut like a knife.

She shoved the key in, started the car, then fastened her seat belt as the engine warmed and her brain started working again. "How long's it been since you last slept?"

"Too long. What's that got to do with anything?"

"We'll get your truck," she said, before she could think of all the reasons she shouldn't do what she was about to do. "Then you can follow me back to my place. I've got an extra bed. You can crash there for tonight. Or for what's left of it, anyway.''

She put the car into gear, but before she took her foot off the brake, she looked over at him, meeting his suspicious gaze squarely.

''I owe you some explanations,'' she said.

He drew in a deep breath, then slowly let it out.

''That you do, Ms....Manion,'' he said flatly. ''That you do.''

Maggie Manion lived in a two-bedroom apartment near the campus. The place was clean, comfortable and as bland and impersonal as only furnished temporary apartments can be.

Rick dropped the overnight bag that he always kept in his truck on the floor by the sofa, then set the long, hard-sided locked case he carried down beside it.

Maggie drew the curtains, then bent to turn on the lamp by the sofa. Her gaze flicked to the locked case.

''You always carry a rifle with you?''

''Not always.'' He didn't feel like explaining himself to a woman who carried a pistol in her pocket and knew how to use it.

Wisely, she didn't press him.

''That bedroom's yours,'' she said, pointing.

"We'll have to share the bathroom. You can go first."

A bed sounded wonderful, but tired as he was, he wasn't ready to go to sleep yet.

"We have to talk."

She didn't look at him as she pulled her gun out of her pocket and set it on the table, then shrugged out of her jacket. Her movements were slow, a little uncoordinated. Maggie Mann—Manion—was almost as tired as he was.

That fact didn't make him feel any more kindly disposed to her.

"We can talk tomorrow," she said, still without looking at him. "I said I'd explain, and I will. Tomorrow."

She started to slip past him. He grabbed her arm and dragged her back.

"It's already tomorrow, and we'll talk right now."

He was stronger, he knew, but she was faster and better trained. If she really wanted to break free of his hold on her, she could. But this wasn't a test of strength, it was a test of wills. And he *had* to know what she knew, or suspected, about Tina.

He wrapped his hand around her other arm and drew her closer.

Even as the questions took shape in his mind, some part of him was aware of her as a woman— a brave, strong, desirable woman who could, as

he'd already discovered, all too easily distract him
without even trying.

This close, she was definitely distracting.

She was slim, but he could feel the firm muscle
beneath the heavy flannel shirt she wore. Her head
would easily rest on his shoulder. If he were to slide
his arm around her shoulders, her body would fit
perfectly against his.

When she tilted her head to look up at him, her
throat curved, open and vulnerable. He could see
the pulse beat at the corner of her jaw. That little
patch of skin would be warm, he knew, and soft.
The secret sort of place where a woman dabbed
perfume when she wanted to attract a man.

Maggie smelled, distantly, of coffee, soap and
weariness, and yet he found himself responding the
same as if she wore some rare, elusive scent.

Her chin was more pointed that he'd realized, her
mouth wider, softer, fuller. Hard, now, yet still desirable.

Her eyes were the dark, secret green of a high
country forest. He hadn't noticed that before.

It angered him that he could notice it now, when
there were more important things to think of.

Frustrated, he gave her an angry little shake, then
let her go.

She winced and grabbed her injured arm.

Rick bit back a curse.

"You're sure that's just a bruise?"

"Yes." That forest-dark gaze came up to meet his worried one. Anger snapped in those dark depths. "Don't *ever* touch me like that again."

"No. I'm sorry. I was out of line."

"Way out of line."

Maggie felt a surge of gratitude for the anger. Anger was so much safer than the confusing, dangerous emotions he so easily roused in her with just a laugh or a casual touch.

Rick Dornier, Ph.D., was in need of a shave, a bath and a good ten hours of sleep. He was worried sick about his sister, and, after the past few hours, Maggie knew he didn't trust her as far as he could spit, but none of it was enough to keep him a safe emotional distance from her, or her from him.

Whatever it was between them, it flared as easily as fire from a struck match, and that scared the very devil out of her.

Her fingers trembled as she raked them through her hair.

She was tired, that's all. The confrontation with Bursey, Nichols and Gage at the station had been even more unpleasant than she'd expected. And her shoulder really did hurt, a low, dull throbbing that she couldn't quite ignore.

Still, she needed Rick Dornier on her side. She wanted the answers to Tina's disappearance almost as much as he did. That's why she'd brought him here. She needed to remember that.

"You were right, you know," she said. "I *am* an undercover DEA agent. Or was, until tonight," she added with a grimace. "Not much cover left now."

She wearily rubbed her arm. "Those two who attacked us still aren't talking, but they both have records. My guess is that they were hired to watch me, maybe break into the Cuppa Joe's, see if they could find anything that might tell them what I know. We surprised them, and they weren't bright enough to stay hidden until we'd gone."

Or maybe they were supposed to keep things simple and just kill me.

That's what Bursey suspected. She'd tried hard not to think about that possibility. In her job, if you spent too much time thinking about what *could* happen, you would never do anything at all.

"You want to sit?" she asked abruptly.

She didn't wait for an answer, just automatically settled into her favorite corner of the sofa, then, when Rick claimed the other end, wished she'd chosen the lone chair, instead. Too late now.

Since she couldn't run, she drew her legs up, then wrapped her arms around them. Maybe he would think it was weariness, not cowardice, that made her curl into a protective ball.

From the corner of her eye, she studied him, the strong, rough lines of his face, the masculine curves and angles of his body, the underlying strength beneath the physical exhaustion.

Her gaze dropped to where his hands rested atop his thighs.

The backs of his hands were broad and strong, carved by the bones and ropey veins beneath the tanned skin. His fingers were long, square-tipped and solid-looking. She would bet his palms were callused from rough outdoor work, but that his touch would be gentle as a whisper when it mattered.

They were strong, capable hands. The hands of a man you could trust.

In her line of work, trusting didn't always come easily. But she would trust Rick Dornier, she thought.

Truth was, she already did. That made the explanations easier.

"I'm here in Fenton because there's been an influx of Asian White heroin into the market in the past few years, and we don't know the source."

"Heroin?" That made him sit up in surprise. "I thought that was out of fashion."

"It was…for a while. Not anymore. People stupid enough to use drugs will go with whatever they can get. And they're always willing to try something new, something 'better.'"

Greg certainly had.

Maggie angrily pushed away the thought. She tried not to think of Greg. It hurt too much.

"There's still plenty of cocaine and meth and all the rest of it out there," she added. "But heroin's back, too. First it was from Mexico, cheap and fairly readily available. Mexican Brown, they call it. Something new for those who like a little variety in their entertainment and weren't around the last time heroin was the drug of choice.

"But then Asian White started finding its way in. The White is cleaner and more potent. It costs more, but that hasn't stopped its spread. The users figure they're getting more bang for their buck," she added bitterly.

"Afghanistan used to be a big producer. A nice cash crop for a struggling farmer, like coca in South America. We've cracked down on Afghani production, but that hasn't stopped the flow of the stuff. These days it's coming out of lots of places—Thailand, Myanmar, India." She shrugged. "It doesn't matter. If you stop production in one place, it will just pop up in another. There's too much money in it not to."

"But why you?" Rick demanded. "Why here?"

"Here, because there's a lot of it on the streets. Me…" She shrugged, trying to feign a professional detachment she'd never been able to master. "I go where they send me, do what they tell me to do, and I'm young enough to fit in with the college scene here."

"And what did they tell you about Tina?"

There was a coldness in him, suddenly. He hadn't budged from his corner of the sofa, but it felt as if he'd moved away somehow, put an impassable distance between them.

She didn't care, Maggie told herself. This was her job, nothing more. There was nothing personal between her and Rick Dornier and never would be.

That didn't make it any easier.

"I got the job at Cuppa Joe's because it's a popular college hangout, but not the sort of place that dealers would be looking for someone like me. I got to hear a lot of gossip, meet a lot of people. It's been…useful."

"*How* useful?"

Her chin came up at the challenge. "*Useful.* That's all I can tell you."

He considered that for a moment. But there was only one thing that really interested him, and they both knew it.

"So where does Tina fit into all of this?"

"Maybe nowhere."

"You don't believe that." It wasn't a question.

"No. But I don't think she's in the middle of it, either." His mistrust stung. That shouldn't matter, Maggie knew, but it did.

She gnawed on her lower lip, weighing what she

could and couldn't say, then tucked her legs under her and leaned toward him.

"We can't prove it—yet—but we think the main source of the White is a professor of art history named Nicolas Jerelski."

He frowned. "Tina's faculty advisor?"

"That's right. She's also one of his student assistants, paid under one of his research grants. Which means she sees him a lot."

"Damn!"

"Exactly. Jerelski is a respected expert on Asian art. He also runs a little import business on the side. High-end original art and reproductions for the home-decorating market. Or so he claims. We think the import business is just a lucrative cover for his even more lucrative drug dealings."

"And you think Tina was involved somehow?"

Maggie shook her head. "I'm pretty sure she didn't know anything about the drugs."

"But…?"

She hesitated, but in for a penny, in for a pound. To hell with what Bursey or her boss would say.

"Bursey thinks she's directly involved in the trade somehow. I don't. But she is bright, inquisitive and trusting. Since she works for Jerelski, there's always the chance that she saw or heard something she shouldn't have."

Rick surged to his feet. For an instant, she thought he was going to hit something. Instead, he stalked to the other end of the room, then spun on his heel and angrily stalked back.

"What about the man who was seen with her?"

"We don't know who he is," she reluctantly admitted. "He might be nothing more than an innocent bystander who happened to be attracted to a pretty girl in a bar."

Rick's jaw hardened. "Innocent bystanders don't run like scared jackrabbits when someone's on their tail."

"No," she admitted, even more reluctantly.

His gaze pinned her to her seat. "I'm going to find her. Whatever's going on, whatever the reason behind her disappearance, she's not a part of it. She's safe somewhere, *and I am going to find her.*"

Chapter 5

The statue, glittering with gold leaf and gemstones, emerged from its nest of swaddling silk and wood shavings like a blood-drenched black Venus from her shell. Diamonds glinted in the eyes of the skulls strung like a necklace around its neck. The silver sword raised in one of the eight hands looked sharp enough to slice a finger to the bone.

"Beautiful! *Beautiful!*" He cradled the thing in his hands, scarcely breathing. Its beauty roused an almost sexual heat in him. "It's even more exquisite than I imagined."

Carefully, he set it down in the light of the green-shaded desk lamp and stepped back to admire the effect.

Eyes wide with awe, his assistant leaned forward to touch it.

He slapped her hand away.

"Don't touch it! It's not yours. Something this perfect, this rare, isn't for the likes of you."

Tears started in her eyes, glistening like the diamonds in the skulls.

He frowned, then sighed, reminding himself of the need for patience for a while longer. But only for a little while.

"I'm sorry. I shouldn't have said that."

He didn't sound as if he meant it, but she told herself it was just the excitement, that he was distracted and she'd interrupted. She knew better than to interrupt. That was the very first lesson she'd learned—never, ever interrupt.

Yet she couldn't keep silent, either. She was just as tense as he was, though not for the same reasons, just as awed by this horrifying, glittering statue that had come so far and at such cost.

"It's very old, isn't it?" she said, because she couldn't bear the silence. Even one of his cutting put-downs was preferable to that.

He was too wrapped up in his new possession to chide her. His gaze devoured the thing.

"Our ancestors were still living in mud-floored huts and picking fleas off each other when the artist that created this was alive," he said, gently touching the thing. His thin, elegant lips lifted in a smile. "And now it's mine."

The hunger in that smile made her flinch and ache with need.

He liked to possess beauty, she knew. It was that fact more than anything else that had convinced her she must be beautiful, too, for he possessed her, body and soul.

"You're going to keep it?" She hated the thought of that thing here, watching her.

"For a few days. Just until my bank in Zurich confirms the deposit of three point two million dollars to my account." His smile widened. "Tax free and untraceable. The very best kind of deposit."

He also liked money. Lots and lots of money.

Delicately, reverently, he traced a line from the tip of the statue's jeweled crown, down the terrible face, the skulls, over the bare breasts and belly.

"Kali," he crooned, more to the statue than to her. "The Divine Mother."

His hand dropped along the angled line of hip and leg shrouded under the carved draperies, down to the bare foot planted atop a carved human skull.

"Hindu goddess of death. Consort to Shiva, god of destruction."

He shifted the thing slightly in the light, his touch as gentle as a lover. "She is…exquisite."

His eyes were like coals burning in the shadowed sockets of his skull. The effect was a trick of the light, she knew—he was such a handsome man she would never have thought such a thing if it weren't for the light and the horrible, glittering goddess with her necklace of skulls that stood on the desk between them.

She shivered, then shifted on her chair, pressing against the growing ache between her legs. She could tell that his breathing had gone shallow and tight, just as it did when he was focusing on one of the more challenging tantric sexual positions that he always insisted they get just right.

At the thought of the sex, the ache within her blossomed. She could feel the wetness and the heat so intensely that she was sure he must be aware of it, too. He had to be. He knew everything—about her, about her needs.

She licked her lips, nervously weighing the risk of punishment for speaking against the possibility of relief.

"Professor?"

He was so absorbed in contemplating the statue that he didn't even bother to look up. "Hmmm?"

"The…the other stuff? It's there in the boxes?"

The need was stronger now, more insistent. Her skin was hot and flushed with wanting.

For the first time since he'd slit open the box containing the stolen statue of Kali, he focused all his attention on her.

"It's there."

She would have laughed out loud in sheer relief, but he took these things too seriously to permit any laughter. She licked her lips instead, savoring the thought of what was to come.

The eight arms of the statue cast a shadow that looked like a large and hungry spider crawling across the polished wood of the desk toward her.

And then *he* was coming around the desk toward her, and she thought he was like that statue, beautiful and terrifying, all at the same time.

She didn't dare move out of her seat. *Couldn't* move, because he was looking at her, weighing her, and she didn't dare risk being found wanting.

Now that he was in front of her, without the desk to shield him, she could see that *he* wanted *her*. The knowledge gave her courage.

He stretched out his hand and stroked her as he'd stroked the statue, brushed her hair behind her ear, traced the curve of her jaw and throat and breast.

"I love your eyes," he said. "They're beautiful. Like water—blue-green one minute, black the next. It's very…erotic. Did you know that?"

She shook her head. Her pulse hammered in her ears, drowning out everything but his voice.

His fingertips lingered on the point of her breast, making her nipple prick beneath the light cotton blouse she wore. She wasn't wearing a bra.

"And your breasts."

She stopped breathing. His fingers tightened

around the nipple, pinching hard. A jolt of heat shot through her. He had always been able to find that perfect point just before pleasure tipped over into pain.

"I love your breasts."

He leaned forward until he loomed above her. His eyes were black holes, his exquisite features starkly outlined by shadows. The light from the desk lamp behind him formed a nimbus of light about his head, making the shadows seem even darker.

His fingers on her tightened, drawing an involuntary yip of pain.

"No one must ever know about *any* of this," he growled.

The pain drew her half out of her chair.

"*No one,* understand?"

"No one will know, Professor. Trust me. I haven't breathed a word to anyone. Not a word. I wouldn't. I *couldn't.*"

She had to force the words out in little gasps. Her chest felt tight, as though her ribs were closing like a vise, squeezing the air out of her lungs and the blood out of her heart. Her skin burned. The aching need inside her made her muscles quiver.

So many needs. So many irresistible needs.

She curled her hands around his wrist and looked up into his beautiful, beautiful face. "Please, Professor. *Please.*"

He smiled then and let go of her nipple.

"I love the way you beg," he said, ripping open her blouse and drawing her down into the shadows with him.

Chapter 6

The ringing of her bedside phone dragged Maggie out of a nightmare in which she was endlessly chasing some nameless, faceless creature that was leading her ever deeper into a swamp where monsters lurked and no one heard her cries for help.

She started up, heart pounding, then grabbed for the phone, still only half-awake.

"You're off the job."

Maggie bit back a snarl. Her boss had never been known for beating around the bush. She sat up straighter in bed.

"The hell I am."

"Bursey called this morning. The men who attacked you last night still aren't talking, but I can't take a chance. Your job in Fenton's done, Manion. Pack up your things and come on home.''

''No.''

To her surprise, he didn't swear at her. In fact, if she hadn't still been half asleep, she would swear he sounded more concerned than angry.

Clearly, she needed coffee.

''I can't afford to risk you, Manion. We've got others in the area. You have done enough.''

She slid out of bed, then grabbed the heavy terry bathrobe draped over the foot of the bed.

''I'm going to look for Tina Dornier, and I'm not quitting until we find her. Somewhere in her disappearance is the key to the whole thing. I'm sure of it.''

''Dornier's not your problem,'' her boss snapped. ''Neither the sister *nor* the brother.''

She shrugged into the robe, wincing at the soreness in her arm. ''I've made them my problem. *Both* of them.''

Maggie shifted her hold on the phone so she didn't catch his reply, but she could hear the irritation in his voice, even though the individual words were unintelligible.

''I'll let you know what I find out, when I find out,'' she said, then hung up before the explosion on the other end of the line could deafen her. She glanced at the alarm clock beside her bed and groaned. Not even six o'clock. The sun wasn't up yet and already the day was going downhill.

The scent of fresh coffee and frying bacon hit her the minute she emerged.

"Oh, God! Heaven!"

And then she stopped, thunderstruck, as her still-sleepy brain awoke to the fact that Rick Dornier was standing in her kitchen clad in nothing but a pair of gray sweatpants and the water droplets that glistened in his hair and the dark curls on his chest.

Maggie blinked, trying to get her brain and her blood pressure to return to normal.

It was a lovely chest. Not the sleek, overmuscled kind that came from hours spent in a health club, but the lean, powerful kind that only an active, physical life produced.

For a man who'd gotten maybe four hours sleep in the past forty-eight, he looked disgustingly alert and cheerful.

She forced herself to breathe, but she couldn't stop her eyes from sliding down that flat stomach with its neat little belly button and the distracting line of curls below it. The curls disappeared beneath the waistband of his sweats, which rode way too low on his hips for her comfort.

Her gaze dropped to his bare feet. Heat stabbed through her.

All these years, it had never once occurred to her that a man's bare feet could be so incredibly sexy. Until now, she hadn't known what she'd been missing.

"Sorry about my state of undress. I set the bacon to cooking while I showered, but it cooked a little faster than I expected." Rick neatly flipped a couple of rashers, then cocked his head in the direction of the coffeemaker. "Coffee's ready. I set out the sugar and a cup for you. I'd have brought you some if I'd known how you like it."

"Sugar." Maggie gave herself a shake, then headed for the coffeepot. "*Lots* of sugar."

She ladled in four heaping spoonfuls, stirred, then leaned back against the counter and took a cautious sip.

"Ahhhh."

She closed her eyes. Savoring the flavor, she told herself. Yet even with her eyes closed, she would swear she could see a half-naked Rick Dornier emblazoned on the backs of her eyelids.

Because she didn't like being thrown off balance, especially not in her own kitchen so early in the morning, she forced her eyes back open.

Now that caffeine was beginning to work its magic on her system, he looked even better than he had two minutes earlier.

"Good coffee." She lifted her cup in acknowledgment and tried not to stare.

"I've already had two cups," he admitted. "I figure another couple along with a plateful of eggs, bacon and toast, and I just might be able to function.''

Just the thought of food before she'd had her first full dose of caffeine made Maggie shudder.

''You sleep all right?'' she asked.

He shrugged. Until that moment, Maggie had never realized just how interesting the gesture could be. There were a lot of muscles involved in that slight, dismissive lift of the shoulder.

On Rick Dornier, they were really interesting muscles.

''Enough to get by for now.'' He glanced at her, then deliberately focused his attention on the bacon. ''Once I have some breakfast and get dressed, I'm going back to that road where we lost him. There's probably nothing to find, but…''

Again that shrug. This time, it wasn't distracting enough. She wasn't quite ready to think about where Tina Dornier might be, or why she'd disappeared. Assuming she'd had any say in her disappearance at all.

Maggie flinched. She definitely didn't want to think about *that* possibility.

''I'm going with you.''

Their eyes locked across the width of the kitchen.

''What's your boss going to say about that?''

''He doesn't approve. In fact, he threatened to pull me off the job and send me back to Washington, ASAP.''

"And what did you say in response?"

"I told him I was going to help you find your sister and that I wasn't quitting until we did."

He cocked his head, studying her. And then he grinned. The grin threw her almost as much as the sight of him half-naked.

"You know, I had a mule once that got that same sort of set to her jaw when she was determined to have her way."

"A mule!"

"I have to admit, she usually got it, regardless of what I might have had to say about the matter."

"Thanks, Dornier," she said dryly. "There's nothing like comparing a woman to a mule to start her day off right."

He gave her a little salute with the spatula.

"Always glad to oblige. If it helps any, it was a darned good mule."

She couldn't help it—she burst out laughing. "I need more coffee."

Rick had to admit to a sense of relief when she turned to fix a second cup.

She looked awfully good in a bathrobe. Better than good—even if it was two sizes too big for her. She looked delicious, actually.

But it was the thought of what was under that robe that really had Rick's blood heating. If he were a betting man, he would bet that underneath all that lumpy terry cloth, she was stark naked.

The thought of Maggie naked was more than a man who was running low on sleep should have to deal with this early in the morning.

Last night, he'd been so tired he could have fallen asleep standing up and never noticed. But he'd noticed Maggie.

When this was all over and Tina was back, safe and sound—

With a soft curse, he cut that thought short.

First, they had to find Tina.

They took Rick's pickup this time. He'd brought his locked rifle case, which he stashed under the second seat in the big crew cab, but Maggie couldn't help noticing he hadn't brought the overnight bag that had held his clean clothes, toothbrush and razor.

Maggie was grateful for the extra space between them on the wide bench seat in front. The sleepy, good-natured banter they'd shared in the kitchen this morning had given way to a grimmer mood, yet she was still as intensely aware of him as she'd been earlier. That troubled her. The last thing she needed right now was to get involved with Tina Dornier's brother.

Involved? She shouldn't even *think* about him. Not in that sense, anyway. But that wasn't easy when he was still close enough for her to catch the scent of him, to hear the soft scrape of his jeans every time he shifted gears.

As distraction, she glanced at the unfamiliar array of what looked like electrical and communications gear that was mounted on the dash—tracking gear for those radio collars they put on bears, she supposed—then focused her gaze on the view out the passenger-side window. At least that way she wouldn't be as tempted to look at him.

Rick had withdrawn into his own thoughts, as well. It wasn't until they were well out of town that he spoke.

"Tell me," he said almost casually. "What did Bursey mean when he said he wanted you out, that you were too emotionally involved?"

The question hit her like a blow.

She scowled at a lightning-blasted pine by the road, thinking fast.

"Relations between us—my agency—and Bursey's people are a little…strained right now," she said, picking her words with care. "They want to put the squeeze on the little guys, the dealers on the street. We want them left alone in the hope that, through them, we'll get the evidence we need to grab the big guys." That was the truth. Part of it, at least.

"Bursey doesn't like waiting, and he doesn't like taking orders from anyone, least of all the DEA."

She shrugged, feigning a casualness she didn't feel. "It's a turf thing."

"A turf thing."

The way he said it made it clear he didn't believe her.

"Yeah. Cops can get awfully territorial, you know."

His glanced at her. Just a quick glance, yet Maggie could have sworn his eyes had bored right through her.

"Bull," he said, very calmly, and very, very firmly. "There's more than just territorial wrangling there. Bursey wasn't talking about the DEA staying out of it. He was talking about *you,* about *you* being too close to it, emotionally. I want to know why."

Tension twisted in her stomach. For a moment, she considered telling him that it was none of his business. But it *was* his business, because it was his sister at the heart of it. If Bursey succeeded in having her pulled off the job, Rick Dornier would be on his own.

She couldn't let that happen.

Maggie drew a deep breath, then slowly let it out.

"Five years ago, my brother, Greg, died of a heroin overdose," she said, struggling to keep her voice controlled and uninflected. "He was using, and he was supporting his habit by dealing. I didn't know. I was a regular cop at the time. I should have seen the signs, but I didn't. Not until it was too late.''

Hadn't seen? Or hadn't wanted to see? Maggie had asked herself that a thousand times since then. She still didn't know the answer.

She swallowed, forcing herself to continue. ''Three weeks after Greg was buried, I quit the police force and joined the DEA.''

Rick glanced at her, then looked away. To her relief, he didn't offer any familiar, worn-out words of sympathy.

''I could see where that might make Bursey think you'd take your work a little more personally than most,'' he said.

That made it a little easier.

''He's right, actually,'' she admitted. ''I *am* emotionally involved. But that just makes me better at what I do. Because I know—really *know*—that what I do matters. Because I know that if I'd done my job five years ago…''

Her words trailed off. She stared out the windshield, unseeing.

If she'd done her job back then—as a sister as well as a cop—Greg might still be alive.

Five years. Sometimes it seemed like yesterday, sometimes an eternity ago.

How long, she wondered, did regret for things not done endure?

''A few weeks ago,'' she continued, ''Bursey

wanted to pull Tina in for questioning. He thinks she's helping Jerelski and that a little pressure would make her crack, give him the kind of information that would allow us to grab Jerelski. I argued against it, said I didn't think she was involved and that picking her up would just make Jerelski and his friends more careful, and therefore harder to catch. I won the argument. Then. But when Tina disappeared…''

"Bursey blamed you."

Maggie nodded. "Yeah."

Rick's lower lip thrust out in a way she was becoming all too familiar with. "I could see where he wouldn't be happy with you. But that doesn't explain why—"

"Greg was out on bail when he died," she said, her throat tight. "The officer who arrested him, the man who was determined to put my baby brother behind bars, was one Phillip T. Bursey of the Fenton police department."

To Maggie's relief, Rick didn't press her further.

The cairn of rocks was right where he'd built it the night before. Judging from the confident speed with which he'd brought them back here, he probably hadn't needed the marker, anyway.

He parked at the side of the road and got out. By the time she reached his side, he was squatted on his haunches, elbows on his knees, studying the dusty, rocky track in front of him.

"Wherever he is, he didn't come back down this way," he said. "There's relatively fresh tire tracks heading in, nothing coming out. Doesn't look like this road's used much, so this is definitely our guy," he added, pointing to a faint impression in the dirt.

Maggie frowned. She'd had enough training in forensics to know he'd been looking for the distinctive tread marks that tires left on dusty or soft surfaces, especially the kind of off-road tires the pickup probably had. Since tread patterns were designed to provide grip to a vehicle in forward motion, it was possible to tell in which direction the vehicle had been traveling when it left a mark. Had the truck come back this way, it would have left marks on top of the first set of tracks, marks that pointed toward the road, not the mountain.

Knowing what he was looking for was one thing, however. Seeing it herself was quite another. All she could decipher from the scuffed dirt was that some sort of vehicle had been over that spot. To her, the rest was dust, rock and gibberish.

Rick gracefully shoved to his feet, then dusted his palms together. "Let's see where he went."

He had the truck in motion before she'd managed to shut her door and fasten her seat belt.

She needed the seat belt and the built-in handhold beside the door frame to keep herself in her seat as Rick bounced and jounced up the increasingly rough, rocky trail. They passed through Ponderosa pines, then higher, into spruce and aspen. The trees closed in about them, but every once in awhile there would be a gap that permitted her to check their location against the topographic map she'd brought.

She'd bought the map when she was first getting to know the area. It helped her keep track of their position now, but it wasn't perfect. According to the map, the trail they were on didn't exist.

Even if she'd had the right kind of vehicle, she would have hated to tackle a road like this herself, but Rick seemed as comfortably at home as if he were cruising down the freeway.

Twice the trail branched, and twice he climbed out to study the signs.

When they got to the third crossing, Rick came to a hard, gravel-crunching halt and slammed his hand on the steering wheel. "Damn!"

The rocky trail they'd been following dead-ended into a paved two-lane mountain road.

For a moment, Rick simply glared at the asphalt strip that cut past them, then he again got out to study the rock-studded dirt track. This time he focused on the few feet closest to the road. When he climbed back in, his jaw was set at a dangerous angle.

"He went right, up the mountain." He glanced at her. "I don't suppose you know what's up that way? Where he might have been heading?"

Maggie shook her head.

"Not for sure. If we're where I think we are, this road peters out a couple miles farther on in a subdivision. You know, one of those places where someone breaks up old ranch property into dozens of forty-acre lots and everybody builds big, expensive houses, then makes a point of *not* knowing their neighbors."

"The perfect kind of place for a drug dealer to conduct his business."

"'Fraid so."

Rick absently drummed his fingers on the steering wheel. "There's always the chance we'll spot a black pickup truck parked in somebody's drive, but assuming we don't get that lucky, the best I can do is check out every single dirt road or drive in the place. Or..."

He eyed her consideringly. "I don't suppose your friends in the agency would be willing to do a little research for us, find out who owns what property, see if there are any connections to known or suspected drug dealers?"

"They might, but it will have to wait until we get back to town—cell phones aren't much good up here in the mountains. Anyway, there's no guarantee they'll find anything. Nothing's led us up here so far. I only know the area because I drove around a lot when I first got here, learning the lay of the land.''

He put the truck in gear. ''You can't find grizzlies if you don't know the range they're hunting.''

Gravel spat from beneath his tires as he pulled onto the road.

They didn't get lucky. No black trucks that they could see, and most of the drives were paved or covered with gravel. The only dirt drive with tracks that might have been what they were looking for led to a house under construction and a battered white pickup with a ladder mounted on a rack at the back. In most cases, they couldn't even see the houses, which were set deep in the heavily wooded lots for maximum privacy. Maggie hadn't realize how hopeful she'd been until they'd circled back to their starting point, no further along than when they'd started. After all these years in law enforcement, she ought to be used to disappointment and dead ends, but when a young woman's safety was involved…

Her hand curled into an involuntary fist. She felt like hitting something. Hard.

Focus, she told herself. *Think.*

''All right,'' she said. ''We go back to town, get some help digging up information on who's up here, see if they can come up with any useful connections. Then we—you and I—go see Jerelski. I'm just a friend, trying to be helpful,'' she added, thinking out loud.

She glanced at Rick. "We've been careful not to let him know we suspect him, so you looking for your sister is the perfect cover. Especially since you talked to some of her other professors yesterday. We've checked out his student assistants, but it wouldn't hurt to check again. And the people connected with his import business. We've been watching them and they all look legit, but maybe there's something we missed. I'll talk to Bursey, see if he can put a couple of his people on looking for Tina full-time. Maybe—''

"*No.*"

Rick's curt objection shattered her train of thought. He pulled off the road and set the brake, but left the engine running.

"How soon do you have to be back in Fenton? For your job at the coffee shop, I mean?"

Maggie glared at him, irritated. She wanted to get *moving,* not sit here and talk.

"Five o'clock. But I left word this morning that I might be late."

"It's still early," he said, clearly thinking out loud. "Only a little after eight. If our guy really came up here last night—and the tracks he left say he did—there's a chance he's still here."

"Yeah, but we don't know where. What are we

supposed to do? Knock on every door and ask if anyone drives a black pickup?''

''When you're looking for bears, sometimes the best thing you can do is sit and wait for them to come to you.''

He twisted around to face her.

''I have an idea, but you're not going to like it.''

Chapter 7

Rick was right. Maggie didn't like it.

She didn't like sitting and she didn't like waiting, and his idea required she do both. That the sitting was done atop a rocky outcrop shrouded by bushes whose branches alternately poked or scraped some portion of her anatomy every time she moved didn't help any.

Worse, the rock wasn't really big enough for two. Which meant that Rick Dornier was way too close for comfort.

For the fifth time in as many minutes, she pushed aside the obscuring branches to get a better view of the entrance to the subdivision where they'd lost their quarry. She'd been on stakeouts before, but this was the first time she'd ever risked a bruised rump and bug bites to do it.

"You're certain he won't spot us here?"

"No."

"No!"

"Chances are he won't spot us. Chances are he won't go down that dirt track where we left the truck, either. But I can't be absolutely certain of either." He shrugged. "Either way, I figure it's a chance worth taking."

Maggie jumped at a sudden stab of memory—of Rick's body, half-naked and still wet from his shower, of the easy play of masculine muscle and bone beneath the warm, damp skin.

She shifted uncomfortably on the too-small rock they shared. "You choose the perfect spot, but the wind shifts and the bear gets your scent anyway sort of thing?"

"That's right."

"But you're absolutely sure you can spot his tracks in the dirt we dribbled across all those driveways?"

He grinned, clearly amused by her skepticism. "I'm absolutely one hundred percent sure of that."

He made it sound so simple.

Maybe it was…for him.

Maggie shifted again, annoyed. She wasn't used to having to depend on someone else's skills like this.

Still, she had to admit they had a better chance
of figuring out which house they were looking for
by using his approach than through any of the meth-
ods she would have used. Always assuming, of
course, that the truck really had come this way last
night, that its driver was the man they were looking
for, that he was still here, and that he really did
know something about Tina's disappearance.

Which was an awful lot of assuming.

*Better than doing nothing, which was what she'd
done for Greg,* she reminded herself grimly.

In the forest behind her, a bird called softly, then
fell silent. The air was laced with the scent of earth
and growing things. It was such a peaceful place
she could almost have managed to forget why they
were there in the first place.

To Maggie's relief, Rick made no effort to chat.
He didn't fidget, either, or check his watch every
three minutes, as she did, or keep parting the bushes
so he could get a clearer view of the empty road
they were watching. He simply sat there, to all ap-
pearances a man with no worries and no desire to
be somewhere else doing something different.

And yet he wasn't a passive lump on the rock,
either. She had the sense that he was, simply, *there.*
In every sense of the word. Alert. Aware. Patient,
not passive.

Though he was leaning back against the rock,
one arm casually propped on top of his bent knee,

gaze seemingly fixed on nothing at all, she would bet her next paycheck that he would be on his feet in an instant if danger threatened. He'd proven that last night in the alley behind the Cuppa Joe's.

Evidently sensing her silent scrutiny, he brought his gaze back from whatever he'd been staring at and turned it on her, instead.

"You okay?" he asked. "Not too uncomfortable?"

"I'm fine," she lied. She leaned forward a bit to avoid the pointed bit of rock that was poking her in the back. "Tina told me once that you two grew up apart from each other, that you'd only gotten back in contact a year ago or so. How'd that happen?"

He shifted a bit, looking for a more comfortable spot. "Our folks went through a really ugly divorce when I was about twelve. Tina was barely a toddler, so she doesn't remember the fights, but there were a lot of them. Dad was a rancher. Mom was a big-city girl who didn't realize that marrying a cowboy wasn't quite the romantic adventure the movies made it out to be. She hated the life and couldn't convince him to change, which made him hostile and her bitter."

He spoke quietly, but beneath the soft words Maggie sensed regret and the remembered pain of a boy caught between angry, warring parents.

"Mom never forgave me for staying with Dad

when they split. I never went to visit them. Tina never visited us.'' He shrugged. ''With more than ten years difference in our ages, it was easy to forget there were two of us, sometimes.''

''Tina didn't forget,'' Maggie said softly. ''She talked about you a lot. Bragged about you, really.''

He looked up, clearly surprised. ''She did?''

Maggie nodded. ''You're a hero to her, you know.''

That seemed to trouble him more than please him. It may have been nothing more than shadows, but Maggie thought he flushed under his tan.

''I'm not much of a hero, I'm afraid,'' he said. ''Since Dad died, I've been so busy running the ranch along with my research and my classes that I was doing good to send her a card for Christmas. But then, a couple years ago, she started calling pretty regularly. Last spring, she asked me down for a visit, and since then we've stayed in touch a little better.''

''That's good.''

He yanked up a stalk of grass. ''Not good enough. I had no idea she was in any trouble, that there was any problem. Maybe if I'd called more often…''

His voice trailed off, the words of self-blame and guilt unspoken.

But they were still there, Maggie knew, even if he hadn't said them out loud. She knew enough about both to know that. She didn't tell him that, though. From firsthand experience, she knew he'd have to come to terms with them on his own.

"Tell me about your brother," he said.

Maggie stiffened involuntarily. "He's dead."

"Not in your memories, he's not."

He said it so gently that she couldn't take offense.

Besides, he was right. For her, Greg *was* still alive and always would be.

"He was funny," she said softly, remembering. "Funny and smart and kind. He and my dad used to go fishing, just the two of them, but Greg always threw back whatever he caught. He couldn't bear to kill the things."

She drew her knees up, then wrapped her arms around them, pulling the memories close. It had been so long since she'd thought about the good parts, the happy times.

"He liked Rocky Road ice cream, nachos and three-cheese pizzas." She laughed. "He *loved* three-cheese pizzas. When he was about five or so, he went off on a kick with knock-knock jokes. Drove us all crazy for months, pestering us with the darned things. Then he got hooked on comic book superheroes and drove us crazy with those. He'd even make his own comic books. Mom thought he might be an artist, but I think it was the stories that appealed to him more than the art."

Beside her, Rick sat quietly, listening, letting her tell the story in her own way without judgment.

He was, simply, *there,* and that was enough. It gave her courage for the rest.

"Our folks died in a car crash when Greg was fifteen. I was twenty-two at the time so I was named his guardian. I'd finished college and joined the police force, which meant I was putting in a lot of long hours, but Greg was old enough not to need a baby-sitter. I figured I could handle it. That we could both handle it."

She frowned at the leafy screen in front of her, remembering.

"At first, everything seemed fine. Greg had had some problems in school even before our parents died, but it was never anything big. My folks suspected that it was mostly because he was so bright that school was pretty boring. He'd cut a class, maybe, or sneak out to cruise with his friends when he was supposed to be doing his homework. Nothing worse than that. Nothing I wouldn't have done at his age, if I'd had the nerve to do it.

"He was already deep into drugs when I realized that things weren't fine at all, that our parents' deaths had shaken him far worse than anyone suspected."

She gave a bitter little laugh. "Ironic, isn't it? I was a cop. I could have told you all the signs to watch for if you suspected someone was using or dealing, but I couldn't see anything with my own brother.''

Maggie looked up to find Rick watching her, eyes dark with compassion and understanding.

''He was nineteen when he died,'' she said, fighting against a sudden constriction in her throat. ''Nineteen years, seven months, six days. I counted, once.''

The sound of a truck coming their way shattered the moment as effectively as a bucket of ice water dumped on her head.

Maggie gasped, then shook herself, struggling to regain control. She ought to know better than to let down her guard like that. The job came first. The job always came first. It had to.

She carefully avoided glancing Rick as she scooched forward to get a better view of the road below.

A dusty black pickup truck exactly like the one they'd followed the night before passed beneath their vantage point, headed into town. From this angle, she couldn't even see the license plates.

''That's him,'' she said, and gratefully scrambled to her feet. ''Let's go see what we can find.''

The truck had come out of a driveway half-hidden in a thick stand of aspen and spruce. Whatever the drive led to was invisible from the road.

Rick parked the truck farther up the road, where

anyone entering or leaving the property would be unlikely to see it.

After her emotional revelations earlier, Maggie had been distant, cold and supremely focused. He hadn't tried to break through her wall of reserve.

The sight of that black pickup had brought the present back with a vengeance. Now all he could think was, *Not Tina. Please, please, please, not Tina.*

He dodged a low branch, then scrambled up a rocky little slope. To the right and slightly behind him, he could hear Maggie moving forward, too. Though she lacked his familiarity with the woods, she wasn't doing too badly at keeping quiet. Her DEA training, no doubt.

He didn't much like the implications, but if she could help him find Tina, it wouldn't matter where she'd learned her skills.

The house was large, the modern five-thousand-square-foot version of a rugged log cabin that probably had three baths and twice as many bedrooms. And a Jacuzzi, Rick thought sourly. Definitely a Jacuzzi.

One side of the house was built into a large rock outcropping on the ridge, which gave the occupants a panoramic view, yet kept the house virtually invisible to anyone on the road below even without the dense screen of spruce and aspen. From what he could see of the recently graveled parking area in front, the place wasn't used much—the drive had a just-raked smoothness that wouldn't have lasted long under heavy use.

A rich man's weekend getaway, he thought, disgusted, and tried not to think about what that might mean for Tina.

There were no cars visible, though the doors on the three-car garage were all shut. No telling what was behind them.

The downstairs windows visible from this angle were uncurtained, but the blinds on all the upper floor windows were drawn, revealing nothing. Good enough. They would manage.

Maggie knelt beside him and silently surveyed the area.

"Doesn't look like anyone's home," she said after a moment.

All the emotion that had been in her voice when she'd talked about her brother was gone. She was a professional now and on the job, her private life and even more private emotions carefully locked away, out of reach.

The message couldn't have been clearer if she'd hung a huge Keep Out sign around her neck.

Right now, that suited him just fine. Later, though…

Later, he reminded himself, was for after they found Tina.

"There's no real cover that I can see," he said.

"But if we come in from around that side of those rocks, we'll be able to get to the front porch without too much risk of being seen from the house."

"And then what? We knock on the door and ask if Tina's home?"

"You got a better idea?"

She frowned, considering, then shrugged. "I'll go first."

She was already halfway there before he thought to wonder if she was carrying her gun.

No one challenged them when they stepped onto the porch. Except for the faint, slightly discordant ring of wind chimes stirred by the light breeze, the house was silent.

Cautiously, Rick peered in the first window. A study or den of some sort. Empty except for the kind of handmade wood-and-leather furniture that would have cost him six months' pay to buy. It didn't look like it'd been used much.

The double front doors were wide slabs of carved pine, also expensive, and securely locked. On the other side, two big picture windows revealed a living room that was furnished similarly to the den, and similarly empty. The dining room, family room and kitchen partially visible at the back of the house seemed equally unoccupied.

If Tina was here, or had been here, he couldn't see any sign of it.

Together, he and Maggie circled the house,

checking windows, jiggling door handles. Nothing, and every door they tried was locked.

When the wall of rock the house was built against stopped further exploration, he went back to the kitchen door and jiggled it again.

Still locked.

Frustrated now, cursing silently, Rick cupped his hands around his eyes and took another, more careful look around. Something about the kitchen had bothered him, but he couldn't figure what.

This second time around, he saw it. There were dishes in the drainer by the sink. He squinted, shifted for a better angle. Two glasses—he could see those clearly. A couple plates. A fry pan. Silverware upended in the holder.

He stepped back, then glanced at Maggie, who was standing at the edge of the flagstone patio, studying the surrounding forest. Her slender body was poised in the relaxed alertness of someone in total control of herself, yet intensely aware of her surroundings and prepared to react instantly, if needed.

Just as she had last night in that alley.

"Hey!" he called. "The DEA teach you anything useful except how to make coffee and shoot people?"

She glanced at him over her shoulder. "What more could you possibly need than that?"

"How are you at picking locks?"

That brought her around. Moving with the distracting, confident grace that was so natural to her, she crossed the patio to him.

"Picking locks?" she said.

Rick caught himself watching her, watching the slight sway of her hips with each step and the way her long legs moved. With an annoyed curse, he dragged his attention back to the matter at hand.

"Yeah. There are two glasses in the dish drainer by the sink, not one. I want to see what other interesting things might be around."

"That's called breaking and entering."

"That's right. But that's not what I asked."

She eyed him, then the gleaming brass doorknob. "I don't suppose you have one of those pocket knives with a million different tools on them, do you?"

Three and a half minutes later, she let out the breath she'd been holding, handed his knife back to him, and pushed the door open.

"If we're lucky," she said, "no one will ever notice those little scratches on the lock."

She stepped through, moving quickly but silently. Rick followed her, every sense on the alert. A quick search confirmed the downstairs was as empty as it seemed.

They moved more cautiously upstairs, working their way room to room, with the same results.

''No one,'' Maggie said, glaring at the empty bunk beds in the last bedroom.

''Not now.''

It was only when he saw the release of tension in her shoulders that Rick realized just how tense and stiff he'd been. Or how much he'd hoped the result would have been different.

''Which doesn't mean no one's been here.'' Her eyebrow arched. ''You're absolutely sure that truck came from here?''

He didn't dignify that with a response.

''All right then,'' she said. ''We go back, room by room, and see what we can find. There may be something, some clue that might be useful.''

They found that two beds—in two separate bedrooms of the six the house had to offer—had been slept in, then tidily made up. The vast Jacuzzi in the master bathroom had a uniform coating of dust along the top, which meant there hadn't been any interesting games held in it any time lately. There were also not-quite-hardened blobs of blue-white toothpaste on one of the bathroom sinks, used towels in the laundry-room hamper and several cans of chili, tuna and green beans in one of the kitchen cabinets. The refrigerator was empty except for a bit of lettuce that had stuck to the rim of one of the crispers and a couple of cans of concentrated orange juice in the freezer.

There was a book on Indian temple art half-hidden under a chair in the empty living room, as though someone had dropped it by the chair, then inadvertently kicked it aside when they'd gotten up. Tina's name was written in a precise, elegant handwriting in black ink on the inside cover.

Maggie stared at the book, desperately wishing she hadn't found it. She didn't want to see the expression on Rick's face when she handed it to him.

She found him in the study. He was standing by the desk, grimly studying some odd, dark, twisted thing in his hand. When she walked in, he set it down on the desk.

"I found that under the desk, at the back. Looked like someone was aiming for the trash basket and didn't realize they'd missed."

The thing was obviously broken off from a painted statue of some sort. The surface was glazed black enamel over what looked like a hollowed out plaster of Paris core. Judging from the smooth finish and fine detail visible on this remaining chunk, the original piece must have been quite striking.

Whatever the statue had represented, it hadn't been a human being.

The figure's head, one half of the trunk and everything below the waist were gone. What was left was two arms and the stump of a third that sprang from what would have been the figure's rib cage. The two hands that survived held curiously wavy, red-tipped gold daggers. Around what remained of the neck was a necklace of grinning, gold-eyed human skulls painted black as the rest.

Maggie grimaced. The figure was…unsettling.

"What is it?"

"A statue of Kali, the Hindu goddess of death." He frowned, then prodded the piece with the tip of one finger, making it rock slightly. "Tina had a replica on her desk last year. It had eight arms, all twisting around it like snakes, and that same damned necklace of skulls. Made my skin crawl just looking at it. She thought it was gorgeous."

Maggie picked it up. The thing looked even less appealing up close. The golden, sightless eyes of the skulls glinted in the light.

"It'd give me the creeps to have something like this around," she said.

He pointed to the hollow center. "Handy place to stash something you didn't want customs to find."

"Yeah. Illegal drugs and gems, especially diamonds, often come into the country this way. The smugglers can't get quite as much in as if they just shipped it in in packets, but it's also a lot harder to find.

"Wouldn't that sort of thing show up on an X ray?"

"It would," Maggie admitted, setting the broken piece back on the desk. "But that's assuming someone has the time and resources to look, which customs generally doesn't. If you had a thousand of these things packed in heavy crates, with maybe a couple hundred in the middle that were stuffed with drugs, there's not much chance anyone would spot the drugs unless they knew in advance to look for them.''

"Who would bother to import that much junk?''

"You'd be surprised. And this is pretty high-priced junk. Some of the stuff Jerelski's business carries sell for hundreds, even thousands of dollars.''

"To each his own, I guess.'' His gaze slid to the book she still held. "What's that?''

When she set the book down beside the piece of broken statue, his eyes darkened. "Tina's?''

"Her name is written on the inside cover.''

Silence. A muscle in his jaw jumped. "Doesn't prove anything, one way or the other.''

"No. Though Bursey's people may be able to find something useful on the statue.''

"Like where Tina is?''

Growing fear lay beneath the anger in his voice. She could hear it.

"No,'' she admitted. "They won't tell us where Tina is. That's something we're going to have to figure out for ourselves.''

Chapter 8

"This is the best I could do on short notice, I'm afraid."

Tina Dornier looked around the living room with its worn, comfortable furniture, the pine-paneled walls, and the shuttered windows, but without really seeing any of it.

"It's fine," she said. "I'll be fine here."

"You're sure?" His voice was rough. With worry, she thought. Worry and something else, something she couldn't decipher and that he wouldn't talk about.

"I'm sure," she assured him. "Don't worry about me."

The look in his eyes said more clearly than words

that he worried about her, regardless. And that, as
much as anything, frightened her all the more.

"But I—"

"Not now," he said, sharply this time. "We'll
worry about all that later. Right now, I've got to go
back. To call my office and pick up your things—
If I can. I'll get them tomorrow if I can't."

"But—"

"Not now, Tina," he said. He traced the side of
her cheek with the tip of one finger.

The light touch made her shiver.

"I'll be back as soon as I can," he said.

And then he was gone and the only sound was
the soft whispering of the pines and the much
louder whispering of her own fears.

Bursey wasn't any happier to see Rick and Maggie than he'd been last night. He tilted back in his
chair, his frowning gaze fixed on them, not the book
or the broken statue on the desk in front of him.

"So, let me get this straight, Manion," he said.
"You want me to spend my department's money
on testing this ugly lump of plaster. A lump that
you claim is a possibly crucial piece of evidence
you admit was obtained by illegal means and is
therefore inadmissible in any court of law in these
fifty united states. But you still want me to test it.
That right?"

Maggie didn't allow herself to so much as blink.

"That's right. Your people have the facilities here. My office doesn't. And since this is a missing person's case—"

"A missing drug dealer," Bursey snapped.

"A missing *person*," Maggie said firmly, before Rick could interrupt. "Which means it falls into your jurisdiction, not mine."

"If you hadn't gotten in the way, we'd have had her already."

Maggie shot Rick a warning look before he could come across the desk at Bursey. He hesitated, clearly angry, then reluctantly sank back in his chair. She turned back to the police chief.

"Look, Bursey. I know you don't trust me, and we both know why. But even you can't deny that my work has helped your department. I can think of at least seven convictions you wouldn't have had without my help. And that's not counting a few that are still pending."

He opened his mouth to object, but she didn't give him a chance.

"Garcia, Roberts, DeLuine," she said, ticking the names off on her fingers. "Asdrubal, Jorgensen, Mar—"

"All right, all right." Bursey angrily waved his arms. "I'll admit, there've been times you've been…helpful."

Maggie didn't dare let her satisfaction show in

her face, but it was there. She'd won. Bursey would help even though he didn't want to.

"So we'll help you look for your missing *person*," he continued. "And while we do, you want my people to dig into tax records to see who owns that little getaway you illegally entered to see if maybe we get lucky and find any interesting connections. That right?"

"Yeah."

"And you want our artist to work with that girl—"

"Woman," she said from between gritted teeth. She might have won, but Bursey wasn't going to make it easy.

"The woman from the bar who identified the guy in the first place. You want *us* to produce a sketch for *you* to use while you run around playing hero. Have I got that right, Manion? You want us to do your dirty work even though you don't want to help us do our job. Right?"

She just glared.

Bursey glared back. "I suppose you know I asked your boss to take you off this case."

She wasn't going to dignify that by admitting anything. Bursey knew perfectly well she did.

Balked of an argument, Bursey swore, then turned his ire on Rick.

"Do you really think you're going to help your sister by breaking the law, Dr. Dornier? Didn't that little incident in the alley last night teach you anything?''

''Yes, I do, Chief,'' Rick said calmly. ''And, yes, it did.''

Maggie was impressed. He might have been at a faculty meeting, for all the concern he showed.

On the other hand, considering some of the tales she'd heard about faculty meetings, maybe he was simply inured to arguments and threats.

''Do you have any idea what you're getting into, Doctor?'' Bursey insisted.

''I'm getting one or two.''

''Well?''

Rick just smiled. It wasn't a friendly smile. It was, in fact, the sort of expression Maggie imagined a grizzly might wear when it was sizing up its next meal.

Bursey swore, then stood so abruptly he set his desk chair bobbing. ''Fine. But if either of you end up bleeding all over the street, don't call us, all right? We're too damned busy to run around cleaning up messes like that.''

Maggie leisurely got to her feet. ''We appreciate any help you can give us, Chief.''

His only response was a growl.

The wind had picked up by the time they emerged from the stationhouse. It carried an icy edge that stung and warned of the winter ahead.

Rick paused on the curb outside to breathe deeply, grateful for the cold, fresh air. Maybe it would ease the dull throbbing of his headache.

Where was Tina? And what in the hell had she gotten herself into?

Maggie halted beside him to fasten her jacket. "That went well, don't you think?"

"Nothing like maintaining good working relations with your colleagues," he agreed sarcastically.

"Absolutely."

He took another breath. Hunting for grizzlies in the middle of a hundred square miles of wilderness was a whole lot easier than looking for one woman. At least in the wilderness, he knew what he was doing.

Still, he had to start somewhere.

And today, at least, he wasn't completely on his own. He'd had his doubts last night, but now, after that little meeting with Bursey, he was glad Maggie was on his side.

"I want to meet this Jerelski character," he said.

"It's a start," she agreed, eerily echoing his own doubts. "Remember, though—you don't know anything about him, or drugs or the DEA. You're just looking for your sister, and I'm just a friend who's helping you, right?"

"Right," he said, and stepped off the curb. "And

if that doesn't work, I'll grab him by the throat and wring the information out of him.''

Maggie shoved her hands in her jacket pockets and followed him toward the truck.

''Works for me,'' she said.

Jerelski still wasn't in his office. The professors in neighboring offices hadn't seen him and didn't know where he was. He wasn't due back for classes or office hours until tomorrow. Check back then, they had said.

Maggie had the feeling that a couple of them didn't want him back, period. Of course, that could simply be the effect of academic jealousy, not something more sinister. Or they could just plain not like the man, no sinister reason needed.

The department secretary wasn't any help, either.

''I'm sorry, Dr. Dornier,'' she said, smiling up at him in a way that was rather more friendly than strictly necessary. Maggie might not have existed for all the attention the woman paid her. ''Dr. Jerelski has class tomorrow afternoon, with office hours afterward. I admit, I'd expected to see him yesterday, or today, at the very least. But he's like most of your professors—comes and goes whenever he pleases.''

She didn't seem to approve of that.

''Do you have a phone number where I could

leave a message for him?'' Rick asked. ''A home
address, perhaps?''

The secretary shook her head. ''I'm afraid I can't
give you that information. The professor's home
phone number is unlisted, and anyway, the university won't let us. Security, you know. They're getting very strict about it these days.''

He nodded sympathetically. ''I understand. It's
the same thing at my university, and believe me, I
do appreciate it.'' He leaned closer, smiling confid-
ingly, and gave her a wink. ''All those students that
want to argue about their grades, you know.''

The woman laughed, clearly charmed.

Maggie suppressed a stab of annoyance.

Rick's smile vanished, replaced by a more somber expression. ''The thing is,'' he said, ''I'm really
concerned about my sister. I'm sure you'll understand. Since she and Dr. Jerelski worked so closely
together, I'd hoped…''

It worked. Three minutes later he was pocketing
a slip of paper with an address and phone number
written on it. They didn't need either—the DEA
had easily dug up that information long ago—but
they'd agreed earlier that it would look odd if he
didn't ask.

Besides, there'd always been the chance they
would learn something useful. They hadn't so far,
but they'd still had to try.

"Thanks," said Rick with another of those dangerous smiles. "I *really* appreciate it."

"Just don't tell Dr. Jerelski I was the one who gave it to you, will you?" the secretary said a little nervously. Now the deed was done, guilt was beginning to war with the persuasive power of Rick's smile.

"Of course not," Rick assured her. "Anyway, I'm sure he wouldn't mind since it's for Tina's sake."

Relief washed across the woman's face. "Oh, yes. Yes, of course. I'm sure Dr. Jerelski wouldn't object for something like that."

Rick gave her one of his business cards with Maggie's cell phone number written on the back in case Jerelski showed up unexpectedly. The woman tucked the card in a holder already stuffed to overflowing with scraps of paper and battered envelopes, but she didn't promise anything.

They were almost out the door when she called them back.

"Since it's for Tina…" She hesitated, then took the plunge. "I just remembered… Dr. Jerelski has a cabin somewhere. A little getaway, you know what I mean?"

Maggie felt her heart skip a beat. They hadn't come across information about a cabin before.

"I don't know where it is, though," the woman admitted. "He only mentioned it once. Well, actually, I overheard him mention in on the phone. He might have gone there, and if it helps you find Tina…''

Rick's earnest thanks eased the doubt in her eyes. Maggie could feel her rather wistful stare follow Rick all the way out of the office. With the promise of another lead to Jerelski in hand, she managed not to let it annoy her.

"Funny," Maggie said once they were out of earshot. "I didn't know you were such a lady's man."

That came out with a little more bite than she'd intended, but he didn't seem to notice.

"I'm not," Rick said.

All trace of the good-natured, smiling charm he'd used on the secretary had vanished. In its place was an unfamiliar, forbidding grimness that hardened the already strong lines of his face. Clearly, Jerelski's sudden absence worried him as much as it did her.

"It's what we in academia call a basic survival skill," he continued. "You either learn how to get on the good side of the admin folk, or you spend the rest of your career scrambling to catch up."

"Ah! It must work. I didn't know about any cabin for Jerelski. That might be handy."

Something in his eyes went bleak and hollow.

"Only if we can find it."

"Now we know it exists, we'll find it. You can count on it."

But would they find it in time? Or would they just be wasting their time when they should be looking for Tina in some other direction?

"Have you been there?" he asked. "To Jerelski's house, I mean?"

She shook her head, grateful to be back on safe ground. It annoyed her that she could be so easily distracted. It annoyed her even more that the secretary's obvious interest in him should have gotten under her skin like that. This was a job, she reminded herself. Rick Dornier was part of it, that's all.

And she would do well to remember it.

"I've driven past it," she said. "But that's all. Coffee shop employees don't generally get invited to dinner by senior university professors. We've watched the place a couple of times, when we thought there might be something going down, but we never saw anyone or anything suspicious. We didn't really expect to," she admitted. "Jerelski's too smart to conduct any illegal business out of his home."

"How about his business?"

"All he's got here is one of those warehouse spaces in a business complex at the edge of town. The stuff comes into West Coast ports on container ships, then the containers get off-loaded onto trucks and brought here, where Jerelski's people break them down into smaller orders for shipping all over the country.''

He gave a soft curse. ''That must be convenient.''

''For Jerelski,'' Maggie agreed dryly. ''Customs have made a point of inspecting some of those containers when they hit port, but…'' She shrugged. ''So far, nothing. It's all been legitimate art imports, so far as they can tell. Which isn't that unusual. There's millions of tons of stuff in millions of containers that come through those ports every year. We could triple the number of customs inspectors and drug-sniffing dogs and it still wouldn't be enough to catch everything coming into this country illegally.''

They were almost to the truck—visitor parking on campus was always a half mile from any place you really wanted to be—when Rick stopped suddenly. So suddenly a student on a bicycle behind them almost ran them over.

The bicyclist muttered something unfriendly as he swung around them, but Rick's only reaction was to grab Maggie's arm and pull her off the path, out of the way.

''What?'' Maggie demanded, irritably tugging her arm free. Every time he touched her, something inside her jumped. This morning in the kitchen had been bad enough, but to be affected by him this easily, when she was supposed to be concentrating on her job, not him.

"You've been looking for drugs," he said, his face suddenly alight with eagerness. "But have you been looking for anything else?"

"Anything else?" Maggie gaped. "Like what?"

"Art," he said. "Stolen art. Did you ever look for *that?*"

"Customs does. All the time. But—"

He glanced around quickly, then pulled her farther away from the path and anyone who might overhear them.

"I just remembered," he said. "The last time Tina was home, she was talking about how big the trafficking in stolen art has become. Billions of dollars a year, she said."

Maggie nodded. "That's right. But it's mostly European art. Old Masters type stuff. And pre-Columbian art from Central and South America, I guess. But we don't generally run into that stuff in the DEA." She shrugged. "The kind of people who traffic in drugs tend to spend their money on fancy cars and expensive jewelry, not paintings they can't hang on their walls."

"Tina said the trade in stolen art from Asia was growing. Fast."

"I don't know about *fast*," Maggie said, "but you're right, it is growing. We just haven't seen any of that around here. Though if we did…"

"Jerelski would be the perfect candidate," Rick finished for her.

"Yeah, he would," she agreed thoughtfully.

"If Tina was going to stumble over anything crooked, it's more likely to be stolen art than illegal drugs."

She frowned, considering the ramifications of what he'd just suggested. It made sense. But where to start looking? And how?

"Let's get your truck," she said. "I need to make a few calls while we're headed to Jerelski's."

Jerelski wasn't at home.

They hadn't expected to find him there, but figured they had to check, anyway.

He wasn't at his place of business, either.

Maggie stared at the door with the words Imports, Ltd. painted on it. There wasn't anything else. No business hours, no description of what Imports, Ltd. did. Nothing.

She'd rung the bell. Twice. If anyone was at the back of the building, they weren't interested in answering.

Rick was peering in the dusty front window, his hands cupped around his eyes to block the sun. The wind ruffled his hair, which was in need of trimming, and the stance dragged his jacket up in the back, giving her a great view of a nicely curved masculine rump and long, masculine legs in well-worn jeans.

She had a sudden sharp mental image of him in her kitchen that morning, his skin still damp from the shower, with his hair uncombed and those worn-out sweats riding enticingly low on his hips.

Deep inside her, muscles tightened involuntarily. Then he shifted a little, angling for a better view, and her breath caught as they tightened again, more demanding this time.

Maggie wrenched her gaze back to the front door. It wasn't any more informative than it'd been two minutes ago, but at least it didn't drag her thoughts down dangerously unprofessional paths.

"Nothing much there," Rick reported, straightening. "A cheap desk, three chairs, a two-drawer filing cabinet, a fax and a phone. There are some papers in an in-box on the desk. Look like invoices from here, but I can't really tell."

"That's it?" To her, her voice sounded a little high and tight, but he didn't seem to notice.

Instead, he nodded. "If Jerelski's into customer service, it's long distance. There's a door through to the back, but it's closed."

They'd circled the building when they drove in. The back was nothing but a long stretch of painted concrete block wall broken at regular intervals with windowless industrial-size garage doors and the windowless regular doors beside them. One door at the far end was open, revealing a couple of vans with Bradley Carpet Cleaning, We Do It Right! painted on the sides.

The only way they'd been able to tell which pair of doors belonged to Imports, Ltd. was by counting. If there was anything of interest in the warehouse area, they would have to try a little more breaking and entering to find it. Maggie had no trouble imagining what Bursey or her boss would say if they did.

"You folks looking for something?"

Maggie spun around to find a gray-haired man eyeing them with suspicion. Mentally, she gave herself a good, swift kick for not being more alert.

"Oh, hi!" she said brightly. "We were looking for Professor Jerelski. Have you seen him?"

The man's expression hardened. "Not lately. What do you want with him?"

The way he said "him" made the pronoun sound like a vulgarity.

"My sister's one of his student assistants," Rick said. He extended his hand. "I'm Rick Dornier. My sister's name is Tina. She's been missing for a couple of weeks and we're trying to find out where she's gone. We were hoping that Dr. Jerelski might have seen her."

The man hesitated, then seemed to decide Rick's direct approach was acceptable, for he thawed visibly.

"Sam Ferguson," he said, shaking Rick's proffered hand. "I run the cabinet shop two doors down." He turned toward Maggie. "And you are…?"

"Maggie Mann." Maggie extended her hand. "I work at the Cuppa Joe's downtown."

That worked even better. The man actually smiled as he shook her hand. "Good place. My wife and I like to drop in for a cup every now and then."

"I'm helping Rick track down his sister. You don't know her by any chance? Tina Dornier? Dark haired, slender, a little shorter than me?"

Sam frowned thoughtfully. "Maybe. I've seen a young woman like that here a time or two, but I've never talked to her." His frown deepened. "I'd suggest you talk to Shana, who ran the place, but Jerelski fired her last week."

She and Rick exchanged looks. "Fired her? Why?"

"Don't know. She came in crying to tell my wife about it. Really shook her, coming out of the blue like that. Jerelski sails in, hands her six weeks' pay in cash and tells her to clear out, just like that. No apology and no explanation. Didn't make sense, either, because she said they were expecting a shipment of that ugly junk he sells, and she always took care of that sort of stuff. Shana was sharp. A real good worker. I'd have offered her a job myself if I could have afforded it, so why would he fire her just when he was expecting more stuff to arrive?''

Maggie tried to keep the rising excitement out of her voice as she asked, ''Do you have a number where we could contact her?''

He shook his head. ''She went back to Chicago to see her family. I told her I'd help her find another job when she got back, but that won't be for a couple of weeks.''

''Oh.'' Rick looked as disappointed as she felt.

''Well, if she comes back early, or you can think of anything that might help us, would you mind calling us?'' Rick handed him another one of his business cards with her cell phone number written on it.

Sam glanced at the card, then frowned again. ''*Dr.* Dornier? You a *real* doctor, or just another college professor?''

''Just another professor, I'm afraid.'' A smile tugged at the corner of Rick's mouth. ''Wildlife biologist, Montana. I study grizzly bears.''

It was amazing how even a small smile like that could light up his face, Maggie thought.

Not that it mattered, she reminded herself sternly. Once Tina Dornier was found and they'd grabbed Jerelski and his people, her job was done. Her boss would drag her back to Washington and the next job, and that would be that. Rick would probably forget her five minutes after she was gone.

If they found Tina safe, that is. If anything happened to his sister, he would probably never forgive her.

Not that *that* mattered, either. Stupid to think, even for a moment, that it did. She had her job, work that was important. Work that made a difference. *That* was what counted. She owed it to Greg to stay focused.

"Grizzly bears, huh?" Sam said, dragging her attention back to the present. He calmly pocketed the card. "Well, if you've got a bear gun, you could do me a favor and shoot Jerelski. He'd deserve it, treating a nice young girl like Shana that way."

Chapter 9

Maggie was looking grim by the time they got back in the truck. Rick wasn't feeling any happier.

He stuck the key in the ignition, but instead of starting the truck, he crossed his arms on top of the steering wheel and stared out at nothing. His shoulders and arms ached with pent-up tension. It felt as if the weight of the world were pressing down on them.

The weight of the world would have been easier to bear than the weight of all the doubts he had.

"I don't like the way things are shaping up," he said. He had to force the words out through a throat gone dry and tight.

"I don't, either," Maggie said. "Things are connecting way too neatly."

That brought him around. "Too *neatly?* What in hell's *neat* about this mess?"

She ticked the points off on her fingers. "First, Tina is seen with a man nobody knows at a place nobody expects her to be, and then she disappears. Within a week, Jerelski is expecting a shipment of something, fires the woman who'd normally receive it and then doesn't show up at the college when everyone there expects him to. His house is shuttered, his business closed and he is no place to be found. There's a possibility that he owns a mountain cabin, but the department secretary doesn't know where and neither the DEA nor the police have ever come across any trace of it. Which is suspicious in itself."

"Suspicious? Why?"

"Because the police and my people have been looking. If there were any property registered in his name in the state besides the house he lives in, we'd know it. But we haven't come across a hint of it. But even if it exists, we may have a hard time finding it."

"The secretary could be wrong."

"Sure. But I don't think she is." A muscle in Maggie's jaw jumped. "Listing property under assumed names or dummy companies is a common way for drug dealers to hide their operations and their profits.''

''And people,'' said Rick, trying to ignore the fear that had been churning in the pit of his stomach ever since Maggie had found his sister's reference book that morning.

''Yes,'' Maggie agreed grimly. ''And people.''

''That house this morning—''

''Could be Jerelski's. It could just as easily belong to someone else entirely.''

''And if it's not his?''

Her eyes mirrored his own doubts. ''If it's not his, then things are even more complicated than they look. And from where I sit, they looked pretty darned complicated.''

''They also might be a whole lot simpler,'' Rick objected. Not because he really believed it, but because he didn't want to believe that Tina's disappearance had anything to do with Jerelski or Jerelski's dirty business. ''Tina's disappearing like this really might be nothing more than a wild fling.''

Maggie didn't dignify that with a response.

''And that man Tina was seen with… If he were associated with Jerelski, your people would know, right?''

Her eyes darkened. ''Not necessarily.''

That wasn't the answer he'd wanted to hear.

Rick curled his hands around the steering wheel

so tightly his nails bit into his palms. This time last week he'd been in Glacier National Park, checking on some of his bears' favorite feeding grounds to see what food was available to them in these last weeks before they went into hibernation.

Seven days, that was all. Only two since his mother had finally broken down and called to tell him of Tina's disappearance.

It seemed an eternity.

Tina had been missing for over two weeks.

"If only I'd gotten to know her better." The words slipped out before he could stop them. Until now, he'd never known how much guilt could attach to the simple words, "if only."

"I should have made more of an effort," he added, remorseless in his self-blame. "I should have gotten to know her friends, paid more attention to her, to her life. If I had, maybe she'd have called me when all this trouble started. I would have come, but she didn't know that. Maybe she wouldn't have disappeared if she'd felt like she had a brother she could rely on, someone who would help her when she needed it."

"Maybe." Maggie let out her breath in an edgy, frustrated sigh. "And maybe not. Even brothers and sisters who grow up together don't tell each other everything. I know all about that, remember?"

He glanced at her and found he couldn't look

away. Her beautiful green eyes had narrowed, turned darker, more challenging. Her square chin was set rock hard; her too-wide mouth was just as firm.

But all that was a facade. Underneath, she was hurting. She'd tallied up the same mistakes and should-haves that he had, and she'd come up with the same gut-wrenching regrets.

Maggie Manion knew all about guilt and the pain that went with it. The only difference was, she'd been all the way to the end of that particular road, and she'd lived with the knowledge ever since.

He hoped to God he never had to come any closer than he was right now.

Something of his thoughts must have shown in his face because her eyes narrowed even further— with concern this time—and she leaned closer. So close he could smell the lingering floral fragrance of shampoo in her hair.

Again his fingers tightened around the steering wheel, but this time it was to keep him from running them through those tangled curls, or smoothing the worried wrinkles from her brow, then tracing the fine, strong lines of her face.

He wanted to touch her, suddenly. Wanted to hold her close and kiss her.

He desperately wanted to kiss her, and because

now was not the time and this was not the place, he deliberately looked away, instead.

"Don't waste time beating yourself up for what might have been, Rick," she said. "You can't change the past."

"*You're* still trying."

That made her flinch. "Which just proves I know what I'm talking about."

He couldn't help himself. He let go of the steering wheel, then shifted just enough so he could reach across the truck's bench seat and pull her close enough to kiss.

It was awkward, and if anyone was watching it probably looked silly as hell for two adults to sit at opposite sides of a truck's seat while trying to kiss.

Awkward and silly be damned. It felt good. It felt right and real.

Maggie was sweet to the taste and warm to the touch. All he could reach was her shoulder, which he closed his left hand around so she couldn't get away. And her neck, which he slid his right hand behind in order to draw her closer. And her mouth, which he covered with his.

That first meeting was just a brush, his lips against hers. He could feel the urgency in him like an engine revving up, starting to race, starting to roar, but, as much as he wanted to, he knew he couldn't let it loose.

He shouldn't even kiss her.

Some small, still-rational part of his brain kept shouting that he should keep things clean and businesslike and simple and definitely *not* kiss her.

The rest of him said to hell with rationality and went back for more.

The second time their lips touched, her mouth opened, welcoming him. He took the welcome and let his tongue slide in to taste her.

She tasted…fine. Even if his head weren't whirling—and it was—he wouldn't have been able to describe exactly what she tasted of, explain how good and right it felt to join with her like this. But then, he didn't need words because his body was doing all right without them. His pulse was pounding, his head felt light and his skin had turned hot.

One thing he was sure of: He wanted more. Lots more. He wanted…everything.

Instead, head spinning, he drew back. But he didn't let her go. He couldn't. And she was so close…

Only inches from his, her eyes widened, the pupils expanding until the green had almost been swallowed up by the black. Her breathing was as quick and unsteady as his—he could feel the slight rise and fall of her shoulder with every breath she took.

His own breathing was none too steady, but he

had just enough sense left to let her go before he couldn't let her go at all.

Stiffly, reluctantly, he straightened back in his seat. She straightened, too, putting even more distance between them. To his relief, she didn't try to edge farther away. She didn't look angry, either. Just…dazed. And a little surprised. And maybe, just maybe, a little sorry that the kiss they'd shared had ended so soon.

Rick dragged his hand across his mouth, then drew a steadying breath.

"Thanks," he said a little shakily.

She drew in a deep, steadying breath of her own. "You're welcome."

"I've been wanting to do that for a while now."

"So have I."

That caught him by surprise.

"But it's not going to happen again. In my line of work, distractions like that can cost a life. Which is why I don't let myself get distracted."

She looked at him as if daring him to protest, then looked away and wrenched her seat belt across her lap. The click of the buckle as it closed sounded unusually loud in the silence of the cab.

Rick couldn't help noticing that her fingers were trembling as she dragged them through those tempting, unruly brown curls.

"We'd best get going," she said.

''Right,'' he said. He fumbled for his own seat belt, then shoved the gearshift into Reverse.

He was half a mile down the road before he thought to ask Maggie where it was they were going.

When Bursey's call came through on her cell phone, Maggie could have kissed the man. Anything was better than the electric silence that hung in the air between her and Rick. Even talking to the irascible chief of police.

''We've got a sketch for you, Manion,'' Bursey said, as brusque as always.

''That's fast. Thanks. We'll swing by and pick it up.''

Out of the corner of her eye, she could see Rick watching her. Her heart rate climbed a notch.

''It'd be more useful if we had a name to go with the face,'' Bursey grumbled.

''Yeah, it would. I'll let you know as soon as we get one.'' *Focus* Maggie told herself. *Think about the job, not the man sitting only three feet from you.*

After a kiss like that, it was impossible to think about anything else.

''What about the house?'' she added. Her palms were beginning to sweat, making it difficult to maintain her grip on the phone.

''Your people find out anything about it?''

"A little. Seems it belongs to some rich German businessman who uses it for an occasional getaway vacation."

"You found that out by checking the tax records?" Maggie asked, startled back to attention.

"Yeah. And calling the German company that was listed as owning it," he added sarcastically.

"German. Then how did Tina and this guy we followed, whoever he is, end up there?"

"Who knows? Maybe they indulged in a little breaking and entering. There's a lot of that going around these days."

Maggie ignored the jibe.

As she told Rick what she'd learned, she was wishing she could ignore him as easily. There wasn't a chance in hell she'd ever manage, though. Whenever he spoke, she found herself watching his lips move and remembering what it had felt like to kiss him.

Rick had never offered violence to a woman in his life, but right now he had a strong urge to grab the idiot lounging on the sagging overstuffed chair in front of him and shake her. Hard.

Just as she had been the first time he'd met her, Grace Navarre, Tina's unhelpful roommate, was more interested in the pot she was smoking than in Tina's whereabouts.

He and Maggie had picked up several copies of the artist's sketch. They'd dropped off copies with Jerelski's secretary, Sam from the woodshop by Jerelski's business and the manager of the Good Times bar, who'd said he'd show it around, but didn't promise anything.

And then they had hit Tina's apartment in the hope they would find Grace home. She'd been home, but she was hostile and not inclined to be helpful.

"You're *sure* you don't know this guy?" Rick insisted, waving the sketch under her nose once more.

"I told you," she said, clearly irritated. "I don't know who he is. I only saw him that one time. I haven't heard from her. I don't know where *she* is or why she's staying away so long. I can't tell you anything else, okay? I don't *know* anything else!"

"But you're sure this is the man Tina was with when you saw her last?" Rick insisted. He was convinced she was lying, but he didn't know what part she might be lying about, or how to drag the truth out of her if she was.

Grace shrugged. A tangle of uncombed hair obscured her face, making it hard to tell what she was thinking.

"Yeah. Pretty sure, I guess. It was two weeks

ago, you know what I mean? I've seen lots of guys since then.''

"But you haven't seen Tina?" Maggie was perched on the arm of the sofa. She looked casual, relaxed, but Rick could sense the underlying tension in her, even from here.

Grace took another drag from the joint, holding the smoke deep in her lungs until she couldn't hold it any longer, then slowly, reluctantly, let it out.

"How many times do I have to tell you, no?" she demanded resentfully. Her voice had an odd little squeak to it because of the pot.

She slumped lower in the chair, then tilted her head back and stared dreamily up at the ceiling.

"I'll tell you one thing." She rolled her head on the chair arm so that she was looking up at him. Her too-thin mouth curved in a sly, taunting smile. "If I'd met the guy, I'd have gone off with him, too.''

"For two weeks? Without a word to anyone?"

Again that damned, dismissive shrug. She delicately waved the joint under her nose, savoring the fumes, then shifted back to staring at the ceiling.

"Sure. Wouldn't be anybody's business but mine, would it?"

Grace had made an art of pretending she didn't care. What Rick couldn't tell was if she was simply defensive, or if she'd pretended for so long that she really didn't care anymore.

"Tina would have worried about you."

Grace's thin shoulders tensed. He could *feel* her hostility and resentment. But was it directed against him? Or Tina?

"Tina worried about *everything*." Grace sneered. "Little Miss Perfect. Drove me nuts, listening to her."

The marijuana's effects took some of the sting out of her venom, but not all of it.

Rather than say something he would regret, Rick crossed to the window and stared blindly out at the tree-lined street, struggling for calm. How in hell had gentle, serious Tina ever ended up sharing an apartment with someone like Grace?

"How'd you and Tina end up being roommates if she annoys you so much?" Maggie asked, eerily echoing his thoughts. She made the question sound casual, as if she were asking for the heck of it, to keep the conversation going.

Grace didn't answer immediately. Rick turned away from the window to find her watching him from beneath that thatch of unkempt hair. He'd seen deer look like that an instant before they fled the wolves that were hunting them.

Underneath that angry, hostile bravado, Grace

Navarre was seriously scared of something…or someone. But what? Or who?

"Were you classmates?" Maggie pressed. "Friends?"

"Nah," Grace said at last, reluctantly. "Her roommate got sick or something, so Tina was looking for someone to share the rent. Just 'til the end of the semester, she said. Which was fine with me. I don't plan on hanging around this dump of a town one minute longer than I have to."

"How'd you find out she was looking for someone? Did you read a notice she posted? Or maybe an ad?"

Grace shook her head. "Nah. She asked me to share."

Rick's jaw dropped. He couldn't imagine his sister ever inviting someone like Grace to share her apartment, no matter how much she needed to cut down on the rent.

Maggie looked as startled by the information as he was. "*She* asked *you?* Why?"

"Friend of mine told her to."

"*Told* her to?"

"All right, *asked* her to."

"What friend?"

A wary light suddenly sparked in Grace's eyes. Then she shrugged and turned her gaze back to the ceiling.

"Just a...friend."

"Anybody we know?" Maggie persisted. "Maybe they could help us figure out where Tina's gone."

Grace was too engrossed in taking a drag to respond. When it was clear she wasn't going to say any more, Maggie tried another tack.

"Mind if we look through Tina's room?"

"You won't find anything," Grace said. "I already looked," she added nastily.

"I'll just bet she did," Maggie muttered as she led the way down the short hall.

It wasn't hard to figure out which room was Tina's—it was tidy, organized and lined with books. Across the hall, Grace's looked like a hurricane had roared through, leaving dirty clothes and full ashtrays lying haphazardly about in its wake. They could smell the stale odor of pot, cigarettes and sweat that hung in the air from five feet away.

With a grimace of distaste, Maggie pulled the door closed, then slipped past him into Tina's room.

Rick remained in the doorway, suddenly reluctant to go farther. There was so much he wanted to know about his sister, but the idea of digging through her personal belongings seemed too...well, *personal*.

Maggie showed no similar reservations. She circled the room slowly, looking but not touching.

And then she circled it again, only this time she opened drawers and dug into their contents, checked behind books, went through the small closet and peered under the bed.

When she came to the desk, which was half-buried under a pile of papers and books and professional journals, she drew out the chair and sat down. Quickly, careful to keep everything in order, she flipped through the material in each stack, then checked the drawers, one by one.

Rick propped one shoulder against the doorjamb and watched her without saying a word. He stiffened a little when Maggie pulled out Tina's checkbook and what looked like a folder of bank statements, but still kept silent. Tina's right to privacy didn't seem very important when weighed against the need to find her and make sure she was safe.

Maggie quickly scanned the check register. "Rent. Groceries. Books. Books. Groceries. Books. Electric bill. Phone bill. Books. Rent. Looks like the only regular deposits are from her student assistantship with Jerelski. And she has a balance of a little over three thousand dollars. Not much, but not bad for a college student."

She tossed the checkbook aside, then started flipping through the collection of bank statements. The farther she got, the higher her eyebrows rose. "Incredible!"

Rick jerked upright, startled. "What?"

"Her accounts always balance. Every single month, right down to the last penny." She shook her head in amazement, then grinned at him. "Now *that's* not normal."

"You scared the hell out me," he growled, settling back against the doorjamb.

She laughed, then put the checkbook and statements back where she'd found them and kept on digging, methodically working her way through the contents of the remaining drawers. She wasn't laughing when she finally sat back, defeated.

"Nothing. Nothing useful, anyway." She rocked back in the chair, frowning thoughtfully. "Your sister seems to have been a very organized young lady, and not just with her checkbook. Her drawers are incredibly tidy, and her files are all neatly labeled and color coded. The books on those shelves seem to be arranged by subject, then shelved alphabetically by author."

She gestured to the untidy stacks of paper covering the desk. "I suspect our friend Grace is responsible for this jumble, because even these piles of stuff are surprisingly well organized. That stack's for general art history," she added, pointing. "This one's for stuff about Indian art—India Indian, I mean. That's for information on art galleries and museums, and that one seems to be notes and handouts from some sort of international art symposium she attended.''

Maggie sat back up straight. ''I have a librarian friend with a passion for organizing things. She'd adore Tina.''

Rick sighed. ''When I asked Tina what she'd like for her birthday last spring, she told me she'd like a couple of good quality file cabinets.'' He slumped down on the edge of the bed, suddenly weary. ''I thought she was joking.''

''So what'd you give her?''

''Diamond stud earrings.''

Maggie gave him a sympathetic smile, then leaned across and patted his knee. ''I'll bet she loved them.''

The warmth that shot through him at her touch wasn't enough to counteract the gloom her words had conjured. Even when Tina had tried to tell him about herself and what she wanted, he hadn't really paid attention. That didn't say much for him as a loving brother who claimed to want to know her better.

What had she thought when she found he'd sent her earrings, not file cabinets? he wondered.

''When we find her, I swear I'm going to buy her all the file cabinets she wants, no questions asked. I'll even rent her an office to put 'em in, if she wants.''

He stood abruptly, suddenly too restless to sit still. He should be out looking for his sister, not worrying about whether or not he'd bought her the right birthday present six months ago.

"Didn't you find *anything* useful?" he demanded.

Maggie frowned. "Not that I can see. What interests me, though, is what I *didn't* find—her planner or scheduling calendar or whatever she used to keep track of things. Someone as organized as Tina is bound to have some kind of a planner."

"She did." He scratched his cheek, trying to drag an image out of his memory. He hadn't paid much attention to those sorts of details, either.

"If I recall right, it was one of those expensive leather-bound things with everything divided up by colored tabs and stuff. Now I think about it, I seem to remember that she carried it with her everywhere she went." He frowned. "I can't imagine her hauling it to a place like the Good Times bar, though."

"That might depend on *why* she went there, and who she was planning to meet."

"We know she came back here and got a bag of her things before she disappeared," Rick objected.

"Do we? Or are we just counting on Grace for that information?"

The implications of that hit Rick like a blow.

Maggie stood, then shoved the chair back under

the desk, taking care to square it with the edge of
the desk as Tina would have done.

"Let's see what else is missing, shall we?" she
said.

His head reeling, Rick followed her to the small
master bath. Evidently Grace hadn't been interested
in the bathroom because everything in sight was
neat as a pin. So far as he could see, the two weeks'
accumulation of dust on the vanity showed no trace
of ever having been disturbed.

Rick watched silently from the doorway as Maggie conducted a rapid check of the medicine chest
and cabinets. She even looked behind the floral
shower curtain drawn across the tub.

"No toothbrush, and the only tube of toothpaste
is still in its box, unopened. Ditto the thing of deodorant. No shampoo or conditioner in the shower.
No tampons or pads in sight."

Maggie's shoulders lowered slightly as if at the
easing of some invisible tension. "Tina wasn't just
snatched off the street. Wherever she went, she
went willingly, and she packed before she left. I
wouldn't trust Grace if I were staring her right in
the eyes, but she wasn't lying about that."

Her gaze locked with his. "There's something
else I didn't find."

"What?"

"Drugs. I found absolutely nothing that would indicate your sister was using or dealing drugs."

"I didn't think you would," he said. But he didn't look at her when he said it—he was afraid she'd see the relief rushing through him if he did.

He also didn't object when she retrieved a small ring of keys from the back of the middle desk drawer, then pocketed them.

"Just in case one of these fits the front door," she said.

When they finally emerged, Grace deliberately draped her legs over the arm of the chair so that her back was to them, then took a long, hungry drag on her joint.

"Didn't find anything, did you?" Her words were starting to slur together, but not enough to cover the hostility in them.

Rick had to stifle a second, more insistent urge to grab the girl and shake her till her teeth rattled. Better to put as much distance between him and her as he could before he gave in to temptation.

He was halfway to the door when he realized that Maggie wasn't following him. Instead, she'd walked right around Grace's chair so Grace would have to look at her, whether she wanted to or not.

"Grace?" Maggie said in a friendly tone. "What's your major in college?"

That startled Grace out of her pot-induced torpor. "Why do you want to know?"

"Just curious."

"Nosey, I'd call it."

Maggie just kept smiling, waiting for an answer.

"Psych," Grace muttered at last resentfully.

"Psychology! Not art?"

"Art!" Grace almost spat the word. "Why would I want to waste my time on something stupid like that?"

"Does your friend study art?"

"My friend?"

"The one who suggested you share this apartment with Tina."

"He's a professor, not a student!" Grace said hotly. "And he doesn't *study*—"

She stopped as abruptly as if someone had shoved a gag in her mouth.

"Yes?" Maggie prompted. "He doesn't…what?"

Grace glared up at her from under a curtain of tangled hair. "Piss off. *Both* of you."

When they finally left the apartment, Grace was blowing marijuana smoke at the ceiling and humming to herself, oblivious to their departure.

Chapter 10

It had to be Jerelski who had arranged for Grace to share Tina's apartment, Maggie thought, not for the first time that night. The pieces fit too neatly, and far too conveniently, for it to have worked any other way.

With practiced ease, she tamped down the freshly ground coffee, then slipped the brew basket onto the espresso machine and locked it into place. She'd been working at Joe's long enough now that she didn't have to think about the work, which left her free to think about other things entirely.

Tonight, there were plenty of other things to think about.

Tina must have stumbled across something.

Drugs, or maybe even stolen art, as Rick had suggested. Given Tina's upright nature and academic focus, stolen art was more likely than illegal drugs. The bit of shattered statuary in a house where she'd been hiding certainly supported that hypothesis.

Or maybe Jerelski just started worrying that she would see or hear something she wasn't supposed to. What better way to find out what your industrious student assistant was up to than to plant a spy in her own apartment? A spy like Grace Navarre, who had no obvious academic connections to him, and who would keep silent and do as he said in return for the drugs he could so easily provide her.

Jerelski must have been aware that he had fallen under suspicion. The stepped-up customs inspections on incoming shipments could have tipped him off, as could have a few visitors to Imports, Ltd. who'd asked a lot of friendly questions but hadn't ended up as paying customers.

The recent arrests and convictions of a number of the local street dealers and a few of the key people higher up the drug ladder wouldn't have made him feel any too secure, either. A couple of those baddies, Maggie was proud to admit, had been grabbed as a direct result of her work here at Joe's. The coffee shop wasn't the usual sort of place for undercover work, but it was popular, and far easier to gossip and pick up bits of information than in the midst of the ear-busting insanity of a place like the Good Times. It was successes like that that made the hardships of the job easier to bear.

She added another dollop of foamed milk to the cappuccino she'd just brewed, angled a chocolate biscotti at the side of the plate, then slid it all across the counter. "That's five-fifty."

She made change from the six dollars the customer handed her, then gave a distracted nod of thanks when the woman dropped the change in the tip jar.

She was only two hours into her shift, but she was having a hard time concentrating.

It hadn't been easy, but she'd finally convinced Rick that they'd gone as far as they could go on the information they had, and that he would do Tina more good by going home and catching up on his sleep than he would by chasing after phantoms. Besides, despite the gaping holes developing in her cover, it still might be handy for her to be able to pass as a friend of Tina's who was trying to help her brother find her.

Rick had reluctantly agreed. That's why he was at her apartment right now and she was here, brewing coffee.

For the first time in years, she desperately wished she could be home.

That in itself was disconcerting. Ever since Greg's death, her work had been her world, her *life*. She'd never minded working a full-time job while undercover because the more hours she put in, the fewer empty hours there were to fill afterward. Until now.

She'd tried to tell herself she was tired, that she needed some time to herself to think through all they'd learned today, but she'd had to admit that was a lie.

She wanted to go home because Rick was there, waiting for her.

Well, all right, he was there, sleeping—three days with little or no sleep had finally caught up with him. When she'd left him there earlier, he'd been fairly reeling with the effects of exhaustion and nerve-wracking worry. He probably hadn't managed more than a bite to eat and maybe a quick shower before collapsing into bed.

But thoughts of Rick Dornier, sleeping, were even more dangerous than thoughts of him, awake. In spite of herself, she kept picturing him sprawled across the bed with the sheets tangled around his glorious, naked body.

Worse, she kept picturing herself naked beside him, her legs tangled with his beneath the sheet, their bodies hot and damp and sated. That was downright dangerous. Just the thought of making love to him was enough to heat her blood and addle her brains.

Bad enough she still remembered every single detail of that kiss this afternoon, every nuance of scent and taste and touch. The details had been whirling in her head, over and over and over, ever since he'd reluctantly pulled away from her, and she'd as reluctantly let him.

But to picture him naked—*them* naked—and in bed together…!

Bursey was right. She *was* too close to her job, but not for the reasons he thought.

Fewer than twenty-four hours had passed since Rick Dornier, Ph.D., had walked through the front door of Joe's, yet she was so raddled by his effect on her that she could hardly think straight. And he wasn't even trying.

It didn't help to know that she affected him pretty much the same, and she wasn't trying, either. In fact, she was trying her damnedest to keep a professional distance between them. Trying, but not succeeding.

She would have to try harder, that's all. Her job was to stop Jerelski and his friends. Helping Rick find his sister was a part of that job. Sleeping with him was not.

She couldn't afford to let hormones muddle her thinking when a young woman's life was at stake.

She couldn't afford to *ever* let them muddle her thinking, because once Tina was safe, Rick Dornier, Ph.D., would be gone.

Once Jerelski and his crew were safely stashed behind bars, she would be gone, too. Back to Washington, then on to her next assignment, wherever that might be.

Since Greg's death, she'd preferred it that way, the change, the constant challenge, the freedom. No strings attached, no commitment to anyone or anything except her job. Given the very real physical risks her job sometimes entailed, it was better that way. For all concerned.

The last thing she needed was to let her own unruly attraction to a man she'd scarcely met get in the way of doing her work or living the life she'd chosen. In fact, she had to admit to a bit of resentment that Rick Dornier had distracted her even this far. After all, home right now was a bland apartment she'd rented furnished. Not exactly the sort of place she ought to be wanting to rush back to. If it weren't for Rick—

"Miss? Miss!" An angry masculine voice shattered her train of thought. "Can I get a cup of coffee, or are you standing there so the floor won't walk away?"

Irritated, Maggie dragged her thoughts back to the present. She forced an apologetic smile. "Sorry! What kind of coffee? Would you like a sandwich with that?"

Yet even as she prepared a cheese-and-veggie sandwich and steamed more milk for the angry man's espresso, Maggie found her thoughts slipping back to Rick Dornier.

It wasn't just sex, she admitted. The sexual attraction between them was potently distracting—no two ways about that. But she'd known sexier, better-looking men than Rick Dornier, and not one of them had ever raised her temperature by so much as a hair. So…why Rick?

It wasn't just their shared experience of guilt and self-recrimination that drew them together, either. That they understood each other had helped to break down the natural barriers between them faster than would normally have happened. But that wasn't enough to explain why she'd been so instantly aware of him the first time he'd spoken, why his smile made something heavy within her grow light and buoyant, why the mere sound of his voice was like honey against her skin, making her nerve ends shiver with anticipation.

God knew she'd tried to hide her reaction, to pretend she wasn't affected. He'd been so worried about his sister that she probably would have gotten away with it, too, if he hadn't been as drawn to her as she was to him.

That he didn't seem any happier about the situation than she was didn't solve anything. If neither one of them could control this attraction thing, how in the devil were they ever going to—

"You heat that milk any more and there won't be any left to foam."

The angry voice once more dragged her back to her job.

"Sorry," Maggie apologized, genuinely contrite. "I'll get some fresh milk."

"Just make the coffee, will you? You start with fresh milk and I'll end up old enough to qualify for Medicare."

You get any ruder and you'll need it, Maggie thought sourly, then felt ashamed of herself.

Amazing what hormones run amuck could do to a normally rational, sensible woman like her.

With a little effort, she managed to finish the coffee and sandwich and pass them across the counter to the still-fuming customer. She paid for his food herself, but even that didn't appease his ill-humor. His back was stiff with indignation as he carried his things to a table at the far side of the room.

Maybe she should camp out in the office tonight instead of going home. She could kick Rick out of her apartment in the morning, then get back to doing her job instead of mooning around like some witless teenager in love with a rock star.

In the end, she gave up the fight, turned over the store to the staff and went home early.

The minute she put the key in the lock, she wished she hadn't. There was an eagerness in her that was almost frightening, a hunger that wasn't sexual, though it had a sexual element to it.

Part of it was relief that the apartment was no longer a few rooms that needed painting and cheap furniture filling the empty spaces. Tonight there was a living, breathing someone in there, waiting for her return.

For the second night in a row, she wouldn't be alone.

He'll be asleep, she told herself. *In the guest room, with the door closed, sound asleep.*

Chances were good he wouldn't hear her even if she slammed the door and clomped across the floor in steel-soled boots. For the past three days the man had been running on worry, adrenaline and far too little sleep. She could probably march a brass band across the living room and back again without waking him.

Reassured, she turned the key in the lock, then quietly pushed the door open and tiptoed through. He'd thoughtfully left the table lamp at the far end of the sofa lit, which was nice of him. The lamp was turned to the lowest wattage, but its soft light was warm and welcoming. Until now, she hadn't realized how little she liked coming back to an empty, unlit apartment.

She glanced at the door to the guest bedroom. It was closed and the crack at the bottom was nothing but a black strip of darker shadows. He was asleep then, as she'd expected.

And that was *not* disappointment she was feeling, either!

Swearing softly, Maggie locked the door, shucked her jacket, then slipped off her shoes. She was halfway across the room when she realized the sofa wasn't empty, as she'd thought.

Rick Dornier hadn't left the lamp on because he was being thoughtful. He'd left it on because he'd fallen asleep before he even reached his bed. A small plate sat on the floor by the sofa, lightly dusted with crumbs from the sandwich he'd fixed for supper. The empty beer bottle beside it was still half-full, set down and forgotten. One of the upholstered pillows had slid or been kicked off the sofa. It must have barely missed the beer and now lay disreputably cocked against one leg of the battered coffee table.

She focused on the details because that was so much safer than focusing on the man sprawled across the sofa.

He'd showered and donned clean clothes before he'd fixed that sandwich, but he hadn't bothered to shave or comb his hair. Now he lay with one arm cocked over his eyes, the other flung over the edge of the cushion so that his fingers curled into a relaxed curve scant inches above the carpet. His stocking-covered feet were propped over the arm of the sofa at the other end, heels close together so that his toes pointed outwards. It couldn't have been comfortable—the sofa was several inches shorter than he was—but he'd probably been too tired to notice. Even asleep, there were shadows under his eyes, and lines of worry etched his broad brow.

But nothing could disguise the lean power of his strong, well-built, eminently masculine body. In some ways, he was almost more dangerously appealing asleep than he was awake. She already knew that he was kind, that he had a sense of humor that was apt to break out at odd times and that he cared deeply about family, and especially about his sister, even though they'd grown up apart. She knew that he was honorable and intelligent and very, very determined, and that, for all his openness, he was still a deeply private person.

Now, asleep like this, his last defenses had come down.

His lashes were longer and thicker than she'd realized. In the lamplight they seemed to glow gold against his sun-bronzed skin.

There was a softer, gentler curve to his mouth than she remembered, and she could have sworn she remembered every detail about it from that kiss this afternoon.

The collar of his shirt was open, revealing the arch of his throat and the slow, steady pulse beating beneath the skin.

His hands were…beautiful. She'd always been drawn to hands for some reason, and she'd noticed his right off. But with him relaxed like this, his fingers curled as loosely as a child's, she had the strangest urge to trace her fingertips across the curve of his upturned palm, then up each finger, one by one. But gently, so as not to wake him.

Her own palms itched at the thought of touching him like that, a touch that would be at once intimate and innocent.

There was nothing innocent about the attraction between them, and nothing innocent about the way her body was reacting to the sight of him, stretched out on her couch as if he regularly took a nap there, as if he were at home.

There was *definitely* nothing innocent about the wild thoughts that the sight of his long, lean body roused in her. Broad chest, slim hips, those long, strong legs. The pieces of him fit so smoothly together—not with the polished perfection of a body sculpted in a gym, but with the easy, powerful grace of a body honed by hard work and long hours on foot in the wilderness.

His skin would be warm, she knew, his hands callused but gentle, his body hard, bigger than hers, stronger.

The needy, hungry heat that washed through her at the sight of him made her palms sweat and her knees suddenly grow weak.

She should go to bed.

Instead, without taking her eyes off him, she sank

down on the edge of the coffee table. She should wake him, she told herself. There were things they needed to discuss, leads to work out, plans to make for tomorrow.

She should send him to bed. He would be a heck of a lot more comfortable there than on the couch.

Then again, maybe it was better to leave all that to the morning, when they were both more wide awake. She'd throw a blanket over him and leave him to wake up when he was ready.

Yes, that's what she'd do. She'd sit here for a moment, relax, let the stresses of the day go. Watch Rick sleep. And then she'd get that blanket for him and go to bed. In a minute or two.

His hand was only inches from her feet. It must be uncomfortable for him, twisted like that. But if she tried to shift his hand, she'd probably wake him up and—

Oh, *hell*. Since when had she started lying to herself?

Her purse gave a loud thump as it hit the floor. The bottom of the beer bottle clattered against the dish as she picked them up and set them out of the way.

His eyes blinked open when she leaned over and kissed him.

''Wha— Uph! Ahhmmmmm…''

He woke up fast and reacted even faster.

His arms came around her, pulling her closer until she was half kneeling, half lying on top of him. And then he pulled her head down to his, drawing her into a kiss that seemed to go on forever.

When she finally came up for air, she was panting and flushed and feeling better than she had in ages.

"You're a heck of a kisser, Dr. Dornier," she said, propping her elbows on his chest and arching back so she could look him in the eyes without her own eyes crossing.

He grinned up at her. "You're not too bad yourself, Agent Manion."

His fingers slid through her hair at the back of her head, gently forcing her back to him.

"Practice makes perfect, you know," he murmured an instant before their lips met.

He tasted of ham sandwich and beer, and Maggie couldn't remember a taste she liked more. Dimly, she wondered how he could breathe with her weight on him like this, but he seemed to be managing all right—the increasingly rapid rise and fall of his chest against her breasts was doing dangerous things to her pulse rate.

She wanted a whole lot more than kisses.

With a low, triumphant growl, she wrapped her leg around his, then rolled him off the couch and onto the floor on top of her.

"So, practice," she gasped, and grabbed his hair and pulled him back to her.

At some point—she wasn't certain how, or when—they managed to shove the coffee table out of the way and drag a couple pillows off the sofa.

They also managed to unbutton buttons, unhook hooks and unzip zippers, but the precise how of it got swallowed up in the storm of need and sensation that engulfed them.

His hands were callused and strong and gentle. His body was as lean and well muscled and beautiful as she'd imagined. And his mouth! That worked miracles as wild as the wildest fantasy she'd ever indulged in.

Somehow, though, it all added up to more than she'd expected. It was almost frightening, how easily he could make her lose control, and how little she cared.

His skin tasted of soap and heat. Her breasts and belly were damp from the trace of his tongue, still tingling with the feel of him long after he'd sampled and moved on. Skin scraped against skin in an erotic tug and slide. She rolled and the tip of one breast brushed against the fine hair of his forearm, making her whimper with the sheer glory of the fire that arced through her in response. The carpet was rough against her back, her side, her knees, her hands, but that only added to the wonder of their joining.

"Now," she said, gasping for air.

"Not yet," he groaned, nipping at the soft skin low on her belly.

"No. *Now.*" She shifted, making him laugh, and rolled him onto his back and claimed him. She gasped at the shudder that wracked her. "Like that!"

She arched, thrust and took him deeper. He arched to meet her, thrust and drove deeper still.

"Like that?" The words were almost unintelligible.

"Like that," she agreed, and wrapped herself around him, and went along for the ride.

It was clumsy and rough.

It was wild and wicked and utterly, brazenly glorious.

She wasn't really sure when her climax claimed her because it seemed to go on forever, then shot higher as he rolled her onto her back without ever losing the rhythm of their joining, then drove against her harder still, damp flesh pounding against damp flesh.

She cried out, blind, deaf, arched violently upward on the crest and slid over into an endless shuddering fall.

She was still caught in the turbulence when he gave a choking groan and strained against her, held for a moment, then slowly collapsed atop her.

* * *

The carpet was something cheap—compact loops
of some manmade fiber in a half dozen ugly shades
of brown and gray—and it was about a half inch
from the tip of his nose.

Which wasn't too bad, Rick decided, considering
his cheek was pressed against Maggie Manion's
shapely shoulder, and the rest of him was covering
most of the rest of her. Of course, it helped that he
was naked, and she was naked, and they'd just
shared some really great sex.

Lazily, utterly content, he stuck out his tongue
and licked the tip along her collarbone. Her sweat-
slicked skin was cooler now. It tasted of salt.

She gave a little murmur of pleasure, like a low
purr at the back of her throat, but didn't bother to
open her eyes. Her arms were wrapped around him,
one hand splayed across his shoulder blade, the
other cupped over the back of his head as if prepared to keep him pinned against her if he tried to
pull away.

Right now, he had absolutely no plans of moving.

He couldn't remember when he'd last felt this
relaxed, or this pleased with himself and life in general. Reality was going to insist on grabbing hold
soon enough. For now…

He shifted a fraction so he could suck on that
soft skin at the side of her throat.

Still without opening her eyes, she gave another little purr of pleasure and turned her head slightly to give him more room.

''Nice,'' she murmured.

''Mmmmm,'' he agreed. He lifted his head to drag the tip of his tongue along her warm skin, over the line of her jaw and all the way to her mouth.

Her smile widened.

There was something very satisfying about a smile on the face of a woman with whom you'd just shared incredible sex.

He propped himself on his elbows so he could look down into her face.

He pressed his hips a little harder against hers. Since her legs were wrapped around his, the contact was…nice. Not quite enough to set things off again—not yet, anyway—but it was definitely nice.

Her arms around him tightened.

He covered her mouth with his.

It was a while before he came up for air. Maybe he'd needed the extra oxygen to his brain, but it only then occurred to him that his weight was crushing her, and that her bare back was being scraped raw by the awful carpet.

''Damn!'' He rolled off her, then helped her sit up. ''You should have told me I was being a jerk.''

He would have stood, but she pulled him around so that they could prop themselves against the sofa, instead. And then she slid into his arms and laid her head against his shoulder, and he couldn't think of much of anything except how good she felt against him, and how much he didn't want to let her go.

"You know this can't last," she said, so softly he almost couldn't catch the words.

"I know." It surprised him, how much that admission hurt.

She slid down a little so her head could rest against his chest, right over his heart, then wrapped her arms around his waist.

"Okay," she said. She might as well have been addressing his navel. "Just so you know."

He couldn't think of anything to say to that.

Instead, he gently massaged her shoulders, then slowly, one delicate vertebral bump at a time, traced down the length of her spine, all the way to the point where the bones disappeared and the soft, tempting swell of her buttocks began. For a moment, he let his hand rest against that firm flesh, savoring the feel of her. And then, one by one, he traced each vertebra back up until his fingers disappeared under the thick, silken curls at the nape of her neck.

His hand curled around the back of her neck protectively.

"Let's go to bed," he said.

"And make love again."

"Yes."

For a moment, they simply remained where they were, so closely entwined that they could have counted each other's heartbeats. Then Maggie pulled free, rose to her feet and extended her hand to help him up.

"Let's go." She grinned. "That is, if you think you're up to it."

And then she raced for the bedroom.

She beat him, but not by much, and laughed when he grabbed her and dragged her down onto the wide bed with him.

Chapter 11

They had breakfast in bed. Coffee, well-buttered toast and each other. The butter clung to fingertips and quickly ended up on even more interesting places.

The shared shower lasted long enough for the water to turn cold and their bodies to heat again with that passionate hunger that roused so easily between them.

But the real world couldn't be kept at bay forever. When Maggie's phone rang, they both tensed.

Clad only in bra and panties, she tossed the jeans she held on to the bed beside the waiting shirt, then walked around to pick up the cell phone from its charging cradle.

"Hello?"

"What's going on? Who *was* that man in the picture you gave me?" The woman's voice on the other end of the line was tear-choked and shrill with panic. "Who *are* you people? What do you *want?*"

"Whoa! Hold on! Who is this?" Maggie demanded.

"Denise. I'm Denise, the art history department's secretary. Remember?"

"I remember, but—"

"I want to know what this is all about!" she demanded. "Dr. Jerelski came in last night, just as I was leaving. I showed him that picture you gave me. Now this! What are you all involved in? Why—"

It took Maggie several minutes to calm the woman down enough so she made sense. By the time she finally got all the details and could hang up, Maggie could feel the muscles in her jaw and neck starting to tighten.

She set down the phone and looked up to find Rick watching her with a gaze so intense it could have stopped a grizzly in its tracks. He'd pulled on his jeans but hadn't fastened them. His shirt still lay on the bed where he'd tossed it down by hers.

The sight of him half-naked just made her feel worse. What in the devil had she been thinking of, to let things between them go this far, this fast? Especially now?

"That was Jerelski's secretary," she said evenly. "He turned up last night, so she showed him the artist's sketch of the man last seen with Tina. She says he—Jerelski—claimed he'd never seen the man, but this morning his office is turned upside down, as if someone was grabbing stuff in a hurry without caring what kind of mess he made. And now he's disappeared again. He's not answering any of his calls and when the campus police drove by his house, they found the back door unlocked and the place in a bigger mess than his office."

She drew in a steadying breath, trying to get her racing thoughts in order. Rick stood there, still as a statue, waiting. A very grim and vengeful statue, she thought, then forced the thought away.

"When they saw the house, the campus cops called their boss, who called Bursey. Bursey's men are at the house now. And the DEA guys are on their way."

"And the secretary?" Rick demanded. "Denise? What did she have to say?"

"She thinks we're involved in something nefarious and have dragged Jerelski into it. And she's really scared that we dragged her in, too."

"Why didn't you tell her you were a cop?"

"Because I'm *not* a cop, but I am in the middle of an important investigation, one we've spent months working on. And I'm supposed to still be undercover," she snapped. "There's probably at least a dozen people around town who still don't know otherwise.''

He grimaced. "You're right. Sorry.''

Maggie forced down her anger. Fighting with Rick wouldn't accomplish anything except waste time.

"She can't help us any further, anyway," she added, more calmly now. "But she did say something interesting. After she discovered the mess in Jerelski's office and called the campus cops, she showed a couple of the other professors the sketch. One of them evidently thought he recognized the guy. He thought he might have met him at some conference or other, but he wasn't sure where.''

"That's not much help.''

"It's something.''

"Enough to find Tina?''

Her temper shot back up. "Don't growl at me, dammit!''

"Well, *is* it?''

The length of the bed was all that separated them, but Maggie could almost see the gulf that was widening between them. For a few short hours they'd been able to forget everything except each other, but now the world had come crashing in and there was no going back.

She'd known it would happen, but that didn't mean she had to like it.

"No, it's not enough to find Tina," she reluctantly admitted. "But it's still more than we had before."

His gaze locked with hers. He looked like a man who wanted to hit something, hard, but had just enough self-control left not to.

"All right," he said at last, each word as hard as bullets. "So what do we do now?"

Maggie grabbed his shirt and tossed it at him.

"We get dressed," she said. "And then we'll decide what comes next."

He should apologize, Rick admitted to himself as he followed Maggie out the door a quarter of an hour later. He was out of line, first to last, and he'd had no right to take his worries out on her.

He wouldn't have if he hadn't been so damned confused as well as frightened.

Last night had been wild and wonderful and satisfying in ways that went far deeper than mere sexual gratification. But that wasn't something he could let himself think about. Not now. Not while Tina was still missing. Especially not when everything they learned about her disappearance flat out scared him more than he already was.

He needed Maggie to help him find Tina. He hated to admit it, but it was true. He'd spent years hunting bears, observing them, studying them, but this was a different and far more dangerous hunt. The stakes were too high to risk making a mistake or to allow himself to be distracted. By anything or anyone.

It wouldn't happen again, he promised himself grimly.

And then he looked up to find Maggie standing by his pickup, staring at him expressionlessly, and he wasn't sure he could keep that promise, after all.

She was so...*real.* So alive and strong and passionate.

Last night, and this morning when he'd awakened, he'd found himself thinking of long-term, of years with her, not days or weeks or even months. The thought had shaken him then, and it shook him now. Not because he didn't want to marry—some day. Or because he thought he would repeat the mistakes his parents had made in their marriage—he didn't.

No, it shook him because it felt like he was betraying Tina by allowing himself to get involved with someone while she was still missing. He owed Tina better than that. He owed her a *lot* better than that.

But he owed Maggie something, too.

If nothing else, he owed her honesty. And he owed himself the same.

Easier said than done when he wasn't sure exactly what it was he was feeling right now.

Maggie must have read something of what he

was thinking in his face. Or maybe she was thinking the same thing, herself.

Her chin came up.

"It's not going to happen again, you know. What we shared last night—" Her mouth thinned, as if she wanted to make sure that whatever she'd been about to say didn't slip out in spite of her. "It's *not* going to happen again."

It was exactly what he'd promised himself, so why did the words sound so wrong?

"No," he said. "It won't happen again."

She flinched as if he'd slapped her, and something in her eyes went bleak and sad.

He felt like he'd been rammed in the gut.

"To hell with this," he growled.

In two steps he'd eliminated the distance between them. But when he tried to take her in his arms and kiss her, she slammed her palms against his chest to hold him at bay.

"No!"

His hold on her tightened. "This is crazy! We're both kicking ourselves for this, and neither one of us deserves it. I wasn't betraying Tina by making love to you last night, and you weren't betraying your brother! Whatever this thing is between us, it has *nothing* to do with them and *everything* to do with us!"

Her jaw set.

"We had sex," she said flatly. "We didn't make

love because we're not in love. We couldn't be! We haven't known each other anywhere long enough to be even close to that kind of insanity! And now's not the time to think about it, anyway, even if we were.''

"No, but—''

She shoved him roughly away "I have a job to do, and so do you. That comes first.''

He was getting mad now. "You're right, it does. But that doesn't mean we have to ignore all the rest. Or pretend there's absolutely nothing between us, when we both know there is. Whether we like it or not, there is!''

She exploded. "What is it with you? Ten minutes ago you were looking at me like I'd crawled out from under a rock. Now you want to declare undying love or something? Well, forget it!''

With a furious curse, she spun around and grabbed the handle on the truck's passenger-side door.

Rick swore. If it hadn't been a heavy-duty truck, she'd have ripped the thing right off.

"It's still locked, dammit.''

She threw him a look of loathing. "Then *un*lock it, dammit!''

"I will!''

"Fine!''

Only he didn't. Instead, he grabbed her again, and kissed her.

For an instant, dimly, he wondered if she would flip him, or knee him or break his neck. Or maybe do all three.

Instead, like a recalcitrant knot that finally lets go, she gave up the fight and leaned into him and kissed him back.

She might as well have clobbered him, because his knees suddenly got wobbly and he couldn't breathe. His pulse rate climbed out of sight. He hardly noticed because the kiss had all the fire and doubt and hunger and fear and the absolute, soul-deep need that lay between them, every bit of it packed into the few seconds or years or however long it was that that one kiss lasted.

He wasn't sure who pulled away first, but he was quite sure his knees would have given out from under him if he hadn't had the truck's still-locked door to lean against.

"I thought I told you never to grab me like that again."

"That's right. You did tell me not to grab you. I remember. But you *didn't* tell me not to kiss you."

"Next time you try it I'll punch you in the nose."

"You can try." What in hell were they fighting about, anyway?

Her eyes weren't bleak or sad anymore. Now

there was a fire in them that he'd swear shot off sparks that were hot enough to burn him.

She poked him in the chest again, harder this time.

"I'm *not* in love with you. And I do *not* get emotionally involved when I'm on the job. Ever. *Especially* not when I hardly even know you."

"There's a first time for everything because here we are, whether we like it or not. Whatever this thing between us, it's not going to go away just because we wish it would."

"It will if I say it will."

"The hell it will."

She opened her mouth to deliver another furious blast, choked and reached for the door handle, instead.

It was still locked.

She gave it a couple of vicious yanks, then threw up her hands in frustrated fury.

"And you *still* haven't unlocked the damn door."

Maggie deliberately didn't look at Rick as he unlocked her door, and she spurned his offer to help her into the truck. She even managed to ignore him as he walked around the truck to open his own door. But it was impossible to pretend he wasn't there when he slid onto the same seat she was sitting on,

Dead Aim

with nothing but three feet of upholstery and empty space dividing them.

That he was working as hard at ignoring her as she was at ignoring him only made it all that much more impossible to pretend that absolutely nothing had happened.

What in the devil had come over her? she wondered, appalled. She'd behaved like a spoiled, irrational child and now she felt like a fool. She'd never, *ever* gone off the deep end like that before. Not at any time, for any reason, and certainly *not* for anything as stupid as this.

She wasn't being fair. She was the one who'd kissed him awake last night. She'd seduced him, not the other way around.

Worse, blaming him for her own lack of control was downright dishonest. Rick Dornier was the kind of man who'd have stopped if she'd said stop, even after she'd started it. Snarling at him now was the same as blaming the other guy for your own mistakes. She'd hated that kind of behavior when she was a kid, and she liked it even less now. Especially since she was the one who was at fault.

She turned to face him. "Look, I—"

"I owe you—" he said at the same time.

He blinked.

She bit her lip, then tried again.

"I'm sorry," she said.

"I need to apologize," he said, before she'd even gotten to "sorry."

"No, you don't," she said. "I'm the one who's behaving like a jerk."

"But I—"

Her frown stopped him cold.

He opened his mouth once, twice. Nothing came out. He snapped it shut and frowned right back.

It might have been easier if he'd argued about it.

"I'm sorry," she said again. Calmly, this time, and very clearly. "I'm sorry for being so rude. I'm sorry for yelling at you. I'm really, *really* sorry for having let things get out of hand in the first place."

Again he started to say something, but she held up a warning finger. Reluctantly, he subsided without a word.

"Neither of us can afford to have any distractions right now. We both know that."

He didn't even try to respond. It might have been easier if he had.

Maggie forced herself to meet his waiting gaze.

"There's one thing I'm *not* sorry for," she said. "I'm not sorry for what we shared last night. Or this morning," she added, suddenly remembering the feel of butter-slick fingers trailing across her bare ribs and down her side.

"I'm not sorry for it," she insisted, "but that doesn't mean it's going to happen again. We can't afford to let it. Right?"

For a moment, he simply sat there, not saying a word, his unreadable gaze fixed on her face. She'd about given up hope of an answer when he let out his breath in an exasperated sigh.

"Right," he said.

"Great." That was the way it had to be, Maggie told herself. So why did it feel like she'd just lost the fight instead of won it?

He started the truck, then let it idle while the engine warmed. "Where to now?"

He might have been asking directions to the bus stop for all the emotion in his voice. Not that it mattered, Maggie told herself. It would make things a lot easier for her if they kept their relationship strictly professional.

If she worked at it, she might even begin to believe it.

"Let's hit Jerelski's office," she said. "I want to find out what's going on. If we're lucky, Bursey's guys will still be there, checking things out."

"All right."

He didn't say another word as he pulled out of the parking lot and slid into the morning traffic that wouldn't be rushing anywhere for the next couple of hours.

She tried to tell herself that was okay, too.

I have a job, she silently reminded herself. He's part of it, but that's *all.* The sex had muddied things up a bit, which was what always happened when you made the mistake of trying to mix your personal life with your professional. She wouldn't let it happen again.

Right now, she wasn't even supposed to *have* a personal life. They were too close to bringing down Jerelski and his friends. She couldn't afford to make a mistake now. Her boss would kill her if she did, and she wouldn't be too happy about it, either.

She sure as heck wasn't happy about losing control like she had there in the parking lot, but that wasn't going to happen again, either. She'd make sure of it.

Think about the *job,* she told herself sternly. Think about Tina, and Jerelski, and this guy that nobody seems to recognize. Except that professor, and he'd—

Maggie bolted upright in her seat.

Wait a minute. What had Denise said? Something about the professor thought he'd seen the guy at some conference of other, right? If the professor was there in the middle of the uproar in the art department, then he had to be a professor of art, too. Which meant a conference, to him, would be something having to do with art. And one of those piles on Tina's desk—

"Turn the car around!"

Rick jumped, startled out of whatever dark thoughts he'd been thinking. "What?

"Turn the car around," she insisted. It was all she could do to keep from bouncing on the seat. "We've got to go back to Tina's apartment. *Now.*"

Chapter 12

To Maggie's relief, Rick didn't ask any questions. He just made an illegal U-turn at the next intersection and headed back toward the campus while she explained.

"Seems awful thin to me," he said doubtfully when she'd finished. "Besides, even if he was at a conference, and that just happened to be the same conference Tina and this professor went to, how are you going to find him? I don't know about the art world, but some of the professional conferences I go to have more people attending than most towns in Montana have residents. And that's just the ones that are registered."

"I'll admit it won't be easy," Maggie said. "But right now, it's all we've got."

Before she could say anything more, Rick abruptly stomped on the brakes, hard enough so the seat belt clamped down, half-strangling her. "What the—?"

"Black pickup," he said, pointing. "And I think it's ours."

Maggie spotted it a moment later. "And that's the parking lot for Tina's apartment complex that he's pulling in to."

His eyes narrowed. "There's binoculars under your seat. See if you can identify him when he gets out."

While she dug out the binoculars, Rick drove past the entrance, then swept around in another illegal U-turn and parked where they had a good view of buildings, the parking area and the truck.

The binoculars were top of the line. Maggie fumbled with the focus, then gave a little crow of triumph.

"Gotcha, you jerk! It's him. It's definitely the guy from the sketch." She adjusted the focus for even better detail. "And he's headed toward Tina's apartment. You are *mine,* buster, all mine!"

Maggie had her seat belt off and her door half open when Rick stopped her.

"Wait! I've got a better idea."

Before she could object, he was out of the truck and unlocking the big metal tool chest bolted on behind the cab. She climbed out after him.

"I need you to stand watch, make sure he doesn't come out too soon," he said as he dug through the chest. "All I need is a couple of minutes. Don't try to stop him. Don't try to talk to him. When you see me back here, come on back. All right?"

"But—"

His gaze locked on hers. "Trust me, Maggie. Please. I'll explain later. Now, just *go!*"

Her hackles rose at the peremptory order, but rather than waste time arguing, she went, moving fast and keeping her head down like someone who was running late and had just discovered she'd forgotten something important.

What in hell did Rick have planned? *Trust him?* Who was the cop, here?

Play it by ear, she told herself, pushing aside her irritation. He wouldn't do anything that would put Tina, or their hopes of finding her, at risk. More to the point, if he hadn't said a word she'd still be doing exactly what she was doing right now. So what was the point in getting pissed?

Maggie swung by the black pickup to make sure there was no one else in it. Empty. She made a mental note of the license plate number and hoped it didn't come too late to help Tina.

Ignoring the temptation to let the air out of one of the tires, she took the path leading to the building next to Tina's. Luckily, the apartments were the kind that opened out onto open walkways rather than closed hallways. The arrangement made spying on someone a whole lot easier.

Once she reached the second floor landing where she could watch both the parking lot and the stranger, she paused and pretended to fumble in her pocket as if searching for her key. And while she searched, she scanned the area.

Rick was strolling across the lot toward that black pickup as casually as if he had all the time in the world. He had something in his hand, but at this distance, Maggie couldn't tell what.

On the third floor landing of the building opposite, the stranger stopped in front of Tina's door. He glanced over his shoulder, then slid a key into the lock, opened the door and, with one last, apparently casual glance to either side, disappeared.

Maggie desperately patted her sides, still searching for the nonexistent key. The gun in her zipped-up jacket pocket was temptingly solid.

What would Mr. Black Pickup do if he walked out of Tina's to find a gun pointed at him by a woman who knew how to use it?

Too bad she wouldn't get a chance to find out.

Rick had disappeared from sight. The parking lot was empty, so far as she could tell. If there were any sounds coming from Tina's apartment, she was too far away to hear them.

Trust me, Rick had said.

She did. That and her own professional training

were all that were keeping her here right now when what she really wanted to do was break down Tina's door, grab whoever it was inside, and wring the information they needed out of him. Drop by drop, if necessary.

The door to a nearby apartment suddenly swung open and a young woman rushed out, her coat and backpack half on, a coffee mug in one hand, the other reaching to pull the door shut behind her.

"I'm going to kill him," the woman muttered, angrily fumbling with coat and pack and coffee. "Switch off the alarm and never tell me. I'm absolutely going to *kill* him."

She gave Maggie a distracted smile as she rushed past, then disappeared down the stairs, still muttering, oblivious to Maggie's cheerful wave. By the time she reached her car, Maggie knew, she would have thought of a dozen different ways to avenge that switched-off alarm clock, and she would have forgotten all about the unknown woman she'd passed on the landing outside her door.

More important, however, anyone watching would think that two neighbors had just exchanged a friendly greeting, and be reassured.

In the building opposite, Tina's door opened a crack.

Rick was still nowhere to be seen.

Maggie threw up her hands as if in disgust at not finding her keys, then headed back down the stairs, heart racing. By the time Mr. Black Pickup got to the bottom, she was standing in the middle of the walkway leading to the parking lot, her back to the buildings behind her, her hands fisted on her hips, scowling at the ground on either side of the path as though searching for something she'd dropped.

She pretended not to notice when he hesitated at the bottom of the steps. It was only a moment's hesitation, just long enough for a visitor to get his bearings…or for someone who didn't want to be noticed to decide how to slip past a stranger planted in the middle of the walk, blocking his escape.

He opted for the brisk, I'm-in-a-hurry approach. Maggie waited until he was almost on top of her before looking up as if startled. Like the woman whose boyfriend had switched off the alarm clock, she gave him a friendly, distracted smile and pretended to turn back to her search. He was six feet away when she called out, stopping him in his tracks.

"Hey! Hi!" She hurried up, beaming and blushing and friendly as all get out. "I know you! You're the guy who was with Tina at the Good Times a couple weeks ago, right?"

She didn't stop for an answer, and she didn't miss the way his body stiffened or his eyes went flat and wary.

"You *are!* I knew it! I couldn't *possibly* forget someone as good-looking as you!" She laughed.

''Lucky Tina! I'm going to have to ask her what her secret is.''

He really was as handsome as Grace had said, sleek and casually sophisticated. The kind of man who ought to be used to exactly this sort of friendly yet pushy come-on from women he didn't know.

''I'm sorry—''

''Oh, yeah. You gotta run. I understand.''

Out in the parking lot, like a man who'd just stooped to tie his shoe or pick up something he'd dropped, Rick gracefully straightened.

Pickup Man was edging away.

Maggie cheerfully, rudely, got closer. ''If I hadn't dropped my damn keys somewhere I'd already be gone, too. Guess it was lucky I did, because otherwise we wouldn't have run into each other like this, right?''

''Right, but—''

''I'm going to give Tina a talking to, keeping you hidden like this!''

She giggled. Pickup Man gritted his teeth.

Behind him in the parking lot, Rick was casually cutting between two cars, yet covering ground fast. He would only need another minute or two.

''Anyway, I don't want to keep you and all, but I thought maybe you'd know where Tina was?''

For an instant, she would swear Pickup Man stopped breathing.

She got closer still, let her voice drop just a little to show she was a concerned friend.

"I haven't seen her for *days*. Not since I spotted you two in Good Times, come to think of it."

He blanched.

"Anyway, she promised to help me with this paper I gotta write, and I really need to talk to her but she hasn't been around, you know? And Grace says *she* doesn't know where she is, so it's really lucky I ran into you because maybe you can help me?"

He shook his head regretfully. "Actually, I've been wondering the same thing because she hasn't been returning my calls. If you see her, would you tell her to call Mike?"

Give the man credit—he recovered fast, and he was a darned good liar.

"Oh. Well, sure." She let her shoulders droop a bit in a disappointment that wasn't entirely feigned. "Call Mike. I'll be sure and tell her that, next time I see her."

"Great. Thanks."

He smiled. One hundred watts of pure masculine sex appeal Maggie thought sourly, though she took care not to let the thought show on her face.

He was already walking away. "Good luck on that paper!" he called back over his shoulder.

It was all Maggie could do to let him go. To hell with her cover. She'd drag him in to "assist" the police in a missing person's case and wring the truth out of him. Drop by drop, if necessary.

And what if he's one of the bad guys and someone's waiting for him to come back? What would happen to Tina then?

She bent to check under a juniper bush at the edge of the walkway.

What if he knows and could lead us to her?

What if—?

Maggie cut the anxious thoughts short. There were way too many what-ifs and not nearly enough answers, and she didn't have time for what-ifs right now, anyway.

She forced herself to return to "searching" for those imaginary lost keys, but out of the corner of her eye, she saw him unlock his pickup and climb in.

What if Tina's joined up with the bad guys?

When he pulled out of the parking lot, he used his turn signal and kept below the posted 25 MPH speed limit.

Maggie's stomach churned. He hadn't looked like the kind of guy who would normally pay attention to turn signals or speed limits.

What if Tina hasn't joined the bad guys, but it's way too late to matter?

The instant he was out of sight, she took off running. If Rick couldn't tail him, she'd boot him out of his own truck and do it herself. She was *not* going to lose the bastard this time! Not even if it meant driving straight up a mountain after him.

Yet even as she ran, Rick's words pounded in her brain.

Trust me. Trust me. Trust me. Trust me.

She let him go!

As he watched the black pickup pull out of the lot, Rick sank back with a sigh of relief. He hadn't been sure she would.

He didn't know much about police procedures, but he was quite sure Maggie would have found a way to take the guy in if she'd wanted to. No matter how much he'd objected. She'd proven that in the alley behind the Cuppa Joe's.

But his way was better.

He punched a couple of keys, studied the computer display in front of him, and smiled grimly. His way was *definitely* better.

An instant later, Maggie wrenched the passenger's side door and flung herself into the cab.

"Go! Go, go, *go*, dammit!" she shouted.

He snatched up the open laptop computer before she could sit on it. "Watch my gear, will you!"

"What the—?" She stared at the computer, openmouthed, then plopped down where it was safe and leaned closer for a better look. "You've got a GPS tracking system?"

"Don't sound so surprised. I track bears for a

living, remember? And close the door,'' he added. ''We don't need the whole world knowing what we're up to.''

Maggie shut her mouth with a snap and did as he said. She was flushed from her dash across the parking lot, and beautiful, and he could have kissed her for having trusted him enough to let the driver of the black pickup go.

''I was afraid you were going to deck the bastard, then drag him in for questioning,'' he admitted as she fastened her seat belt without taking her eyes off the laptop's screen.

''I thought about it,'' Maggie admitted. ''I really, seriously thought about it. But this is better.''

He frowned at that tantalizing blinking light that indicated the truck's location and tried to ignore the knot of tension in his gut.

''Maybe. At least we won't scare him off by tailing him too close.''

''What'd you do? I saw you disappear behind his pickup, but that's all I could see.''

''I fastened one of the satellite radio collars I use for bears around a strut under his back bumper. He's not going to see it unless he gets right up under the truck.''

''And the computer?''

''Stashed behind the seat with the rifle and some other equipment. I carry it with me most of the time, just in case I need it.''

She shook her head in amazement. "You use a satellite tracking system, yet you don't even own a cell phone. Seems crazy to me."

He shrugged. "Most places I go, cell phones don't work. GPS does. The computer runs off the cigarette lighter. This cable here connects it to the receiver there," he added, pointing to the electrical equipment mounted on the truck's dashboard.

"But the screen's only showing a topographic map. No streets. No roads."

He picked up the folded maps they'd used the day before and tossed them in her lap.

"Trucking companies go for road maps. Biologists don't. You did just fine yesterday, and this is a whole lot easier. There's more than enough information there that we can compare maps where we need to."

He picked up the computer. "I'll drive, you navigate. And you can tell me what happened out there while you do."

"Deal." She eagerly took the computer from him. "Come to Mama, baby. Come to Mama."

He released the emergency brake and put the truck into gear. He was glad Maggie was here beside him. Glad and very, very grateful.

"Let's go see where this fellow's leading us."

"Yes. Let's." Maggie shifted the computer on her lap so he could see it, too, "Mama's coming to get you, Mr. Mike, you lying jerk," she crooned softly, eyes avid as she watched the blinking light moving steadily across the screen. "Mama and the Bear Man are definitely coming to get you."

The man called Mike led them to another heavily wooded subdivision, this one closer to town. The houses were older and smaller, but just as secluded as the luxury getaways. Street signs and numbers on mailboxes gave them an address.

To Maggie's relief, her cell phone worked. While Rick looked for someplace to pull the truck off the road where it wasn't likely to be spotted, she picked a comfortable spot in the shade of a gnarled old pine that was off the road and out of sight of the drive to the house. Then she called the location in to Bursey's office.

To her even greater surprise, Bursey himself came on to the call while an assistant tracked down information on the house.

"Bear collars?" he said when she'd finished explaining. "You aren't planning on going in there alone, are you, Manion?"

"Of course not."

The man might be difficult, but he wasn't dumb. "A wildlife biologist, even one who plays with grizzly bears for a living, is not adequate backup, dammit."

"I just want to see who's in there, find out what

we're dealing with. I'm not planning on storming in, guns blazing.''

"You might have to." He sounded tired. Angry and tired. "We had a murder here last night, Manion. Guy named Jason Taublib. That ring a bell?''

Maggie sucked in her breath. "You know it does. We figured he was Jerelski's main man, that he got the stuff into the system. Your people agreed.''

"Right. And this morning Jerelski's office and house were found turned upside down, as if someone packed in an awful big hurry.''

"I heard about that.''

"You would." Oddly, the comment sounded more admiring than annoyed.

Maybe she needed her ears checked.

"We don't have any more information," he added. "Not yet, anyway. But even without knowing more, it pays to be cautious. This fellow you followed—''

"Might be inclined to shoot first and ask questions later.''

"He might." Bursey swore tiredly. "It'd help if we knew where he fitted into this whole thing. Him and Dornier's sister.''

"Yes," Maggie agreed curtly. "It would.''

She didn't want to think about Rick's reaction when she told him.

"I don't know if— Hang on." Bursey must have covered the mouthpiece on the phone because all she could hear was a murmur of voices. The words themselves were too muffled to make out.

Her own thoughts were whirling. Taublib murdered. Jerelski missing, his business closed. All the work she and the others had been putting in to break up Jerelski's business was clearly beginning to pay off, but right now that didn't matter nearly so much as their increasingly urgent need to find Tina.

Bursey came back on the line. "The house you're looking at is a vacation rental. We got lucky—the owner handles the rentals, and he was home when we called."

"We're due for a little luck."

"Yeah, well... About a week ago, a fellow named Fritz Hoenig took it for a month. The thing rents for a thousand a week plus deposit." Bursey paused significantly. "Hoenig paid cash. In advance."

The bottom dropped out of her stomach. "That's a lot of cash."

"It is for cops like you and me. It's not very much if you're in some other line of work." Again Bursey paused. "Take a look around, Manion, see what you can learn. But don't *do* anything, all right? You find anything, you let me know. We'll get warrants and backup up there, pronto."

"Thanks. In the meantime, you'll tell my people?"

''They're already in. What?''

That last was directed to someone in Bursey's office. Once again Maggie could hear the sharp-edged murmur of urgent conversation, but she couldn't make out the words.

Bursey came back on the line. ''I've got to go, Manion. But you be careful, you hear? I don't much like you, but I wouldn't like to see you dead.''

''That makes two of us, Chief.'' She cut the connection, then just stood there, blindly staring at nothing. ''That makes two of us.''

Rick appeared a few minutes later, strolling along the road like a man out for a tranquil walk. Only someone who looked closer would notice the hard set of his jaw or the alertness alive beneath the calm exterior. Rick Dornier, Ph.D., was not a man she'd want to meet in a fight, but he was someone she'd be very, very glad to have at her back if one developed.

Or in her bed anytime.

Heat licked through her at the thought, raw, distracting and elemental.

Shaken, she tamped it down, then pushed her way back through the bushes to the road. He came to a stop beside her.

''I left the truck around that bend in the road.'' His gaze sharpened. ''What happened while I was gone?''

Maggie told him Bursey's news. She kept it short, but he had no trouble connecting the dots.

She'd hate to be the one on the receiving end of the thin-lipped, hard-eyed look he shot at the silent drive and the hidden house.

"Guess we'd better go see who's home," he said softly.

Maggie unzipped the jacket pocket where she kept her gun. "Guess we better," she agreed.

As they had before, they kept to the cover of the trees, paralleling the drive. It was a short drive and ended in front of a neat green frame house with no garage. The only vehicle in sight was the black pickup.

Rick fought against the urge to simply race across that open yard, break down the door, then storm in. He probably wouldn't have won the battle if the front door hadn't swung open just then and the driver of the black pickup hadn't stepped out.

The expression on the guy's face had Rick's insides turning to ice. What he saw there was fury, grim determination and fear. Especially the fear.

To hell with Maggie or with anyone who might still be in the house, watching them. The bastard was not getting away this time.

Pulling out the specialized pistol he'd brought from his truck, Rick stepped out of the trees and into the fellow's path.

At the sight of Rick, and the pistol he held, the man stopped dead.

Behind him, he could hear Maggie curse, then shift position so she could cut the guy off if he decided to run back toward the house. Or shoot him if he pulled out a gun.

Rick didn't worry about that. His attention was fixed on the man himself standing frozen, right there in front of him.

If there was anyone in the house, Maggie would have to deal with them.

"Where is she?" Rick kept his voice steady, but it cost him an effort.

The other man didn't even try to pretend he didn't understand. "Gone."

"Where?"

"I don't know."

Rick fought back the sudden fear churning in his gut. The hollow, haunted look in the other man's eyes wasn't the expression of a man who feared for his own safety, but of a man terrified for the safety of someone else. A man terrified for *Tina*.

"Is there anyone else in the house?"

"No."

He didn't move, didn't change expression as Maggie, gun up, darted into the house, but Rick had the sense that something in him hardened, as if he'd just determined on fighting his way out of this, if necessary, rather than talking.

For an instant, Rick considered jumping him now, before he had a chance to go for a gun.

"You're Rick Dornier, aren't you?" the man said. "Dr. Rick Dornier, Tina's brother?"

"That's right. Who are you? And where's my sister?"

The stranger didn't bother answering either question.

"You do know she's dealing drugs, don't you?" he said instead.

"Tina? Tina's dealing *drugs?*" Fury squeezed Rick's throat. He'd throttle the bastard right now if he didn't need to know what he knew, first.

"No. *Her.*" The man cocked his head in the direction of the house where Maggie had disappeared, but kept his hands down and away from his sides to indicate he wasn't reaching for a weapon.

"Maggie?" Rick stared at him in disbelief.

"From the Cuppa Joe's, right? Maggie Mann? She's some sort of informant. A go-between."

"You're crazy!"

"No, I—"

"All clear!" Maggie came around the side of the house, her gun held loosely at her side rather than in a two-handed grip in front of her. "There's nobody else. At least, not now."

Her angry gaze raked the stranger. From the expression on her face, she would happily have shredded him bare-handed, but the need for information stopped her, too.

"Meet DEA agent Maggie Manion," Rick said softly. "Undercover agent Manion, actually."

"DEA!" That shook the man far more than the guns had.

"That's right. Who are you?"

"Fritz Hoenig." He regrouped fast. "I'm a private investigator specializing in tracking stolen art. There's a business card and ID in my wallet, hip pocket."

Maggie handed her gun to Rick, then warily retrieved the wallet. She was almost disappointed he didn't give her an excuse to take him down. He didn't move as she riffled through his wallet's contents, either.

Through it all, Rick just stood there, that odd, long-barreled pistol of his still pointed at the stranger's chest. He looked like he was seriously hoping Hoenig would give him an excuse to use it.

"Nice wad of cash." At a guess, Maggie would say two or three thousand, but she wouldn't swear to it. She wasn't used to seeing quite so many hundreds in one man's pocket.

"The ID says Fritz Hoenig. Berlin." She glanced up. "You're German?"

"Dual nationality, German and American. I grew up in Germany, but went to Harvard like my father. Yale for graduate work."

There was a faint trace of accent in his English, but it was very faint. If the ID hadn't said Berlin, she probably wouldn't have caught it at all.

Maggie flicked the edge of the plasticized, holographic card. "Nice picture. If the ID's fake, it's a good one."

She frowned at the business card. "Hoenig and Bruck, Art Retrieval Specialists. Business cards are *very* easy to fake."

"You can check. Interpol knows me. I've worked with them often enough. You can also confirm my identity with some of the people I've worked with in Washington, among other places."

He listed a few names and titles. Some of them she recognized. A couple she knew personally. Or, rather, she'd met them a time or two. They were way too high up the ladder for her to be talking about a really personal acquaintanceship.

If Hoenig was telling the truth, and she was beginning to think he was, the man was well connected. Unfortunately, the people he was connected to did not spend their days wandering through art galleries; they spent them chasing down some of the world's really unpleasant people.

She didn't much like what that might mean about Hoenig's presence here, or his connection with Tina. She deliberately didn't look at Rick because she was afraid of what she'd see in his face, in his eyes. He didn't have to recognize Hoenig's con-

nections to know they boded no good for Tina—
the titles alone would have been enough to warn
him.

Maggie pocketed the wallet and retrieved her gun
from Rick. "I'll keep the wallet. And unless you
can produce Tina Dornier for us, pronto, you'll ac-
company us to town so we can verify your ID."

Rick reluctantly lowered the pistol, but didn't
bother returning it to whatever pocket he'd gotten
it from.

"And while we're on the way," he growled,
"you can tell me what in hell has happened to my
sister."

Maggie had the strangest feeling she now knew
what a grizzly sounded like, just before it devoured
its prey whole.

Chapter 13

They strapped Hoenig's hands behind him with duct tape that Rick dug out of his tool chest, then belted the man into the front passenger seat so Maggie could keep an eye on him from the back seat while Rick drove. They'd already called Bursey's office asking for a priority ID check. His secretary had promised to get someone on it, pronto.

Right now, pronto didn't seem anywhere near fast enough.

Before they'd left, Rick had searched the house and surrounding area more carefully, but the second search hadn't revealed any more than the first: Tina's clothes, books and the few personal items she'd brought with her were still spread out as though awaiting her return. The graveled drive and paved road beyond wouldn't have held any footprints.

A trained search-and-rescue dog might have found some trace of her. To the human eye, however, there was no hint of where she'd gone, or why, or when she might be back.

Her absence made their interrogation of Hoenig just that much more pointed.

"Tina attended a lecture I gave on international art theft at a conference in Denver a few months ago," Hoenig said. "She knew my company specializes in the recovery of stolen art, so when she began to suspect that her academic advisor was importing more than cheap knockoffs, she contacted me."

Rick snorted. "She thought of someone based in Berlin first? There's no one in all these fifty united states and Canada who could have done as well?"

Hoenig went still. Even with his eyes on the road, Rick could see the flush that rose to the man's face. His own upper lip trembled in an incipient snarl. He could guess what came next.

"She came up after my lecture," Hoenig said softly. "We got to talking, I invited her to dinner..." He shrugged. "We spent a week together in New York, just before the semester started. I've already bought tickets for her to come to Germany in December."

Tina was involved with him?

Not my business, Rick reminded himself harshly. But he couldn't prevent the stab of guilt that he hadn't known, that Tina hadn't felt she could share that part of her life with him, and that he hadn't thought to ask.

"Why hide out?" Maggie demanded. "Her disappearing like that just attracted attention, rather than the reverse."

Hoenig shifted uncomfortably in his seat, but froze when Maggie yanked back on his seat belt.

"Keep still and answer my question. Why hide out?"

"At first," he said, "all we intended was to spend a few days together. Her work for Jerelski had been some sort of academic cataloging of important pieces of Indian and Asian art held in various museums and private collections around the world. By chance, she got to know the young woman who clerked in Jerelski's import business—"

"Sarah."

Hoenig shook his head. "Not Sarah. Shana."

Rick sensed Maggie relax, just a little. It didn't prove that Hoenig really was who he said he was, but it was something.

If Hoenig caught the change, he was smart enough not to show it. "Anyway, the two of them got to talking about what they did, and that's when

Tina realized there were some odd coincidences in timing between the reported theft of a piece of art and Jerelski's receipt of merchandise. She told me, and I did some checking of my own. That's when I flew out here.''

"Just like that?"

He didn't pretend to misunderstand. "There's usually a very fat finder's fee for anyone who provides information that leads to the return of an important piece of stolen art. And it's very good for our business to be there first. Besides, it was a good excuse to see Tina.''

Rick's grip on the steering wheel tightened—many more days like this and he'd turn the thing into a pretzel—but he managed to keep his mouth shut and his eyes on the road. *Not his business.*

It was crazy, but he'd swear he could hear Maggie's soft voice, somewhere in the back of his brain, chiding him for being a fool. She knew all about guilt and obligation, and how crazy they could make you.

She also knew about loving. And making love. And laughing. That alone would have made him fall in love with her, forget about all the rest.

Fall in love?

The thought drew him up short. Not now! For God's sake, not *now!*

With a silent curse, he forced his attention back on Hoenig.

"Tina had already e-mailed me a copy of the data she'd assembled for Jerelski," he was saying. "She'd talked Shana into making copies of some of his business records, too. Data files, invoices, that sort of thing. Probably not admissible in court, but enough to get me started. Only…it disappeared."

"What do you mean it disappeared?" Maggie demanded.

"Tina had packed a bag with clothes and books and things, enough for a couple days away, then left it there in the apartment while we hit the Good Times bar that first night. She swears she put a copy of her research notes plus the stuff Shana gave her in the bag with everything else, but it wasn't there when she looked for it later on."

"Why the bar?" Rick interrupted. "That's *not* the sort of place Tina would choose for a night on the town. Why go there?"

"She wanted to point out someone she thought might be managing Jerelski's dirty work because she figured I'd be able to find out more about him."

"And did you?" Rick had a sick feeling in the pit of stomach that he knew what Hoenig was going to say next.

"Yes. I can't prove it—yet—but I think she was right. The man's name is Jason Taublib and—"

Maggie sucked in her breath.

"What?" Hoenig twisted around to stare at her. "You know Taublib?"

"Taublib's dead," Maggie said flatly. "He was found last night, shot. And Jerelski very conveniently seems to have disappeared."

Rick couldn't see the expression on her face, but he figured he didn't need to. He figured he knew what it was, the same as he'd known what Hoenig had been about to say.

For a moment Hoenig simply stared at her. And then he carefully shifted back around to stare blindly out the windshield, oblivious to the fact that his hands were still duct-taped behind him.

For the first time since they'd followed him from the Good Times bar, Rick felt a certain sympathy for the man.

Right then, Fritz Hoenig didn't look particularly handsome, but he sure as hell looked dangerous. Frightened, though not for himself, and very, very dangerous.

Fritz Hoenig was who he'd said he was. The confirmation came through fast enough, and from enough important sources, that Maggie suspected he was probably a lot *more* than what he said he was. Interpol, maybe, working undercover in that cozy little office in Berlin. The job of "art retrieval specialist" would make a very handy cover for any number of special operations.

While they'd waited impatiently at the Fenton police station for the search-and-rescue dogs that were being brought in to look for Tina, he'd filled them in on the rest of the last two weeks.

The weekend getaway that he and Tina had originally planned stretched to a week, then two after his contacts in Washington confirmed that both Jerelski and Taublib were under suspicion, but for drug-dealing, not art-smuggling. His contacts had asked him and Tina to stay low and not throw a monkey wrench in the drug investigation, and they'd reluctantly agreed.

That those same contacts hadn't informed her superiors in Washington of his existence was, in Maggie's opinion, yet more proof that Fritz Hoenig was far more than some fancy, jet-setting P.I. Unfortunately, finding out just how much more would have to wait until they found Tina.

One thing Hoenig *hadn't* promised his contacts was to ignore the disappearance of the best leads they had to Jerelski's illegal art dealings—the files and invoices that Shana had copied for Tina. Grace was the obvious suspect, but though Hoenig had searched the apartment three separate times, he hadn't found the missing documents.

A few nights spent tailing her, however, had revealed something Tina hadn't suspected and Maggie and Rick had only guessed—Jerelski was providing Grace with drugs in exchange for information.

"Jerelski must have realized that Tina's research was a double-edged sword." Hoenig absent-mindedly rubbed his wrist where they'd cut the tape away. "Which is why he put Grace in the apartment to spy on her in the first place."

"Junkies make bad spies," Maggie objected. "Their loyalty is to whoever can provide the next fix."

All the while he'd been talking, she'd been running yet another computer search in a desperate effort to track down that mountain cabin Jerelski might own. So far, she'd found exactly what Bursey's people had found—absolutely nothing.

"True, but he wouldn't have needed to depend on her for very long. He must have known you were closing in on him and his operations. And if Tina's information is correct, his art theft ring was getting big enough to be attracting some major attention, too. He probably planned on one or two more big scores, max, before he dismantled what he could and walked away from the rest."

"But he's a respected university professor," Rick objected. "An internationally known expert in his field. I'm no criminologist, but I do know academics and their egos. Jerelski sounds exactly like the type that craves the fame and glory as much as the money."

With each word he seemed to get angrier and angrier, but Maggie knew, better than anyone, that the anger was only there to cover up the fear. The waiting had been by far the hardest on him because there'd been nothing for him to do except listen to Hoenig's tale, and worry, and wonder if any of this would have happened if only he'd somehow done something different somewhere along the way.

She'd had to fight against the urge to go to him and offer what small comfort she could. He'd deliberately avoided looking at her. She'd tried to tell herself that she was grateful for his restraint, that it was better to keep a safe emotional distance between them.

So far, she hadn't come close to believing it.

Hoenig didn't seem to notice Rick's suffering. Perhaps because he was suffering, too.

Anyone could see that he was deeply in love with Tina Dornier. His fears for her safety had given him a haunted, hungry look and added a dangerous edge to his voice, but they hadn't broken through the wall of reserve that seemed a natural part of him. Yet.

"Jerelski is not going to happily walk away from the status and respect he's gained as a professor and art expert," Rick insisted. "He may have no choice now, but that's just going to make him angrier. And more dangerous."

"Maybe," Hoenig said. "I've run into more than

enough art experts to know you're right. But given the chance, I don't know of many who would choose the glory over the gold. A few million dollars can be an effective balm for even the biggest egos.''

Rick simply growled and stalked away to the window. The view outside was of a half dozen parking spaces and the building's Dumpster, but Maggie knew he wasn't looking at the view. There could have been a dozen gorgeous women out there dancing naked in front of the window and he wouldn't have noticed them, either.

The computer in front of her beeped, dragging her attention back to the records search the system had just finished. She sighed. Still no hit. And she couldn't think of anything else that might work for Jerelski. Not a single blinking thing.

Concentrate on what you *can* do, Manion, she told herself sternly, not on what you can't.

She arched her back, stretched, then settled back in front of the computer. Forget Jerelski. Maybe he hadn't owned a cabin after all. Maybe that vague comment the art department secretary remembered had referred to someone else's cabin. But whose?

Maggie scowled at the patiently blinking cursor. Not another professor. There would have been no need for Jerelski to cover up the fact that he'd been another professor's guest. A friend? Nope. Drug dealers and art thieves didn't have friends, they had associates.

Okay, then. Who was Dr. Nicholas Jerelski's nearest and dearest associate?

The answer hit like a bolt of lightning.

Her fingers were typing the name even as it formed in her mind. She hit enter, then waited, scarcely breathing, as the system worked its magic. When the record finally came up on the screen, she stopped breathing altogether.

Then she saw the legal details that identified the property. Subdivision, lot number, section, township and range. For a moment, she thought she'd gotten confused, that she hadn't remembered the other information right, but when she pulled out the slip where one of Bursey's people had written down some of the same details, she realized that she wasn't confused after all.

Still, just to be sure…

She opened the paperbound, oversized book of maps that someone here had loaned her when she'd asked for a computer so she could run the search. The battered, dog-eared atlas included both roads and topographic detail for Fenton county. It only took a minute to find what she was looking for.

When she finally started breathing again, she looked up to find both Rick and Hoenig standing there, staring at her like men who'd just spotted their best hope of salvation.

"What's the matter?" Rick asked.

Hoenig was more direct. "What'd you find?"

She printed out a copy of the property record, then grabbed the atlas as she stood.

"Jason Taublib owned a two-bedroom cabin," she said. "And it's located less than a quarter of a mile from where Tina disappeared."

They didn't wait for the dogs and handlers. Maggie gave the dispatcher the details, but they didn't wait to hear if the call for the police backup she'd requested went out, either. Not even to confirm that the backup was to come in silently, without lights and sirens.

Since several units had just been called to the scene of a major traffic accident with fatalities, and another two were tied down with a fight that had broken out at a bar on the edge of town, the dispatcher had warned them it might be a little while before anyone could respond to their request for assistance. They didn't waste time worrying about that, either.

It was sheer luck that they didn't get stopped for speeding.

"I don't believe in coincidence like this, dammit!" Hoenig complained as Rick slowed to a mere ten miles over the speed limit coming into the sprawling, heavily wooded mountain development. He was leaning over the front seat, eyes fixed on the road ahead and clearly wishing he were driving, instead.

Rick didn't respond. He'd been tempted to open the door and pitch the SOB out of the truck ever since he'd climbed in. Blaming the man for Tina's disappearance didn't make any more sense than blaming himself, but a little physical violence would have been a welcome relief right about now.

"Coincidences happen," Maggie said. "Tina must have gone out for a walk and spotted Jerelski or his car."

"Or he spotted her," Rick said grimly.

"We'll check out the house from the trees, then divide up and get as close as we can," Maggie said. "I'm in command— And no arguments about it," she added sharply when Hoenig started to protest. "As it is, I'm going to catch hell for letting two civilians assist and for not waiting for backup."

"You don't have any choice in the matter." Rick slowed, then cautiously turned into the drive of the house Hoenig had rented. Hoenig's truck was still there. So far as he could see, nothing had changed since they'd last been here.

"Doesn't look like anybody's home."

Hoenig was already slipping into the house when he and Maggie slid out of the truck. He reappeared in the open front door a few moments later and unhappily shook his head.

The bottom dropped out of Rick's stomach. Until

this moment, he hadn't realized how much he'd been hoping that they'd find Tina here, miraculously returned, as though she'd just stepped out for a little stroll and taken her time coming back.

Maggie nodded, then opened the atlas she'd grabbed from the station and spread it out on the fender of his pickup.

Despite the urgency of what lay ahead, Rick couldn't keep himself from studying her, just for a moment.

Now that they were actually *doing* something, the weariness that had shadowed her eyes and slowed her step earlier had vanished. Her jaw was set, her mouth had thinned into a determined slash, and her eyes glittered with a determination that boded ill for Jerelski or anyone else who might want to harm his sister.

The very sight of her reassured him and eased some of the fear that had been gnawing at him since this desperate search for Tina had begun.

He'd often worked with women before. Talented, intelligent, determined women as capable and professional as their male counterparts. Women he'd trusted and respected and relied on.

But never, until now, had he relied so much on anyone. Never had he trusted so far, or been so sure that his trust was not misplaced.

The dying breeze teased at Maggie's tousled curls, blowing them against her cheek and brow.

Distracted, she brushed them off her face. When the breeze tossed them back, she simply ignored them and frowned down at the map spread out in front of her.

Raw energy almost sparked off her, and for a moment, a very brief moment, Rick could almost feel sorry for Jerelski and anyone else who stood in her way.

"If we go by the road, there's always the chance that we'll be spotted," she said, her gaze still fixed on the map. "Judging from this map and from what we've seen of the area, it wouldn't be that hard to work our way through the trees. No ridges or steep gullies or anything like that. But this area's been developed for awhile, which means there'll not only be a house on every lot, it means there'll be fences and dogs and God knows what else that we'd have to get past."

"And all without alerting anyone to the fact that we are here," said Hoenig dryly.

"Exactly."

"Which means we go up the road."

Maggie nodded unhappily, then flipped the atlas shut. "And try damned hard not to be recognized."

She looked up then to meet the German's level gaze. "Jerelski's seen the police sketch of you. He knows you're here in Colorado. If he has Tina—"

Her gaze swung to meet Rick's. He stifled his

own doubts and gave her a small, almost imperceptible nod of understanding and support.

Reassured, she turned back to Hoenig. "If he has Tina, then he probably also knows that you've been working together. And if he knows that, then he'll be expecting you to come after him. And her."

Hoenig's sculpted upper lip curled in a snarl. "I hope so. And if any harm has come to her—"

"She's fine," Maggie said quickly. "She has to be. Jerelski needs to know what she's learned and who she's shared that information with. He can't afford to harm her."

At least, not until she's told him everything she knows. But after that, she's expendable.

None of them said the ugly truth aloud, but Rick could tell that each of them were thinking it.

"Jerelski can't afford to harm her," Maggie repeated firmly. "And we can't afford to waste time worrying about things that—for right now, anyway—are completely out of our control."

She dug into her jacket pocket and pulled out a black knit cap. "Have you got a hat, Fritz? Something to hide your face? Maybe a different jacket? Anything to make you less recognizable?"

"In the house. Give me a minute."

Rick watched him go. Once Hoenig had disappeared inside the house, he turned to find Maggie studying him, her gaze level, her expression unreadable.

"I don't suppose there's any chance you'll stay here, wait for our backup," she said.

"No."

She nodded. "I didn't think so. Promise me one thing, though. Promise me you won't bring that weird pistol of yours, okay?"

He opened his mouth to object.

She held up her hand before he could say a word. "I'm quite sure you're a good shot—probably a heck of a lot better than me. But I'm a law enforcement officer. You're not. If I shoot Jerelski, there'll be an inquiry. If you shoot him, all hell will break out. So just leave the pistol, okay?"

He sighed, then reluctantly agreed. "Okay."

"Not that we're shooting anyone, of course," Maggie added hastily. "But just in case."

"If he's hurt Tina, I won't need a gun," Rick said grimly. "I'll tear him limb from limb, instead."

That made her blink, then grin. "That's okay, then. We can probably handle that."

He couldn't help himself. Rick lowered his head and kissed her.

It wasn't a passionate kiss, and it didn't last very long, but it was still potent enough to make his breath catch.

Reluctantly, he pulled away. Not far, but far enough. Far enough that he could see that her eyes had gone wide and dark. Her lips had softened, parted. He wanted to kiss her again, but didn't.

"Thank you, Maggie Manion," he said softly. "For everything."

And then he straightened. "You and Hoenig take the road. You're going to need someone coming in from behind, so I'll go through the trees."

She nodded, and backed away. Not far, but far enough.

"All right. You might as well tear the map out of that book. You won't do us any good if you end up behind the wrong house."

The three of them compared their watches and agreed on times, signals and what each would do, and how.

"This is reconnaissance," Maggie reminded them. "We're not planning on taking the place by storm."

"At least not until we know where Tina is and make sure she's out of the way," Hoenig said.

Maggie didn't try to argue. She checked her gun one last time, slipped it back in her pocket, then started up the drive. Hoenig fell into step beside her.

Rick waited until they were both out of sight, then retrieved the gear he wanted from the truck, checked that everything was in order, and set out through the trees after them.

Chapter 14

They didn't see anyone along the road, and so far as Maggie could tell, no one saw them. Even though they weren't dressed like runners, they tried to make it look as though the two of them were just out for a little hard road work by jogging the whole way.

By the time they ducked into the trees that screened Taublib's cabin, Maggie was breathing fairly hard. Hoenig hadn't even started to sweat.

"You need to get more exercise," he said as he studied the small cabin that was their target.

"I'm getting plenty just by sneaking up on houses around here," Maggie shot back, annoyed.

She scanned the house and the trees around it.

"Is that Jerelski's SUV parked around the side of the house?"

Hoenig nodded. He hadn't glanced at her once since they'd left the road. "One door at the front. Maybe another around the back. Two bedrooms, right?"

"Right. I figure it's those two small windows on the side. The bathroom would be where that even smaller window is between them. My guess is the rest is a combined living and dining room with open kitchen. That's the usual arrangement in places like this."

"Agreed." This time he glanced at her. "You want the front or the back?"

"Back. But we've got another ten minutes until Rick can work his way around."

Hoenig recognized the warning in the comment but chose to ignore it.

"I'm not waiting. Dornier's a biologist, not a cop. You and I are trained for this sort of thing. He's not."

He pulled a small and very deadly looking gun out of his pocket, then turned to scan the silent house once more.

"Every minute we wait is another minute that Tina is at risk. I'll give you five minutes to get in place, then I'm going in the front."

With that he was gone, moving fast and keeping low.

Maggie gave herself the satisfaction of one heart-felt curse, then pulled her gun and started around the other side.

There was a back door. From her vantage point in the woods behind the house, Maggie couldn't tell if the door was locked or not. But she could see movement in the room beyond.

The windows on this side of the house weren't very big. With the lengthening late afternoon shadows it was hard to tell exactly what was going on since no one in the house had been thoughtful enough to turn on a light.

Heart pounding, ears straining for any sound that could tell her what was happening inside, Maggie took a chance and dashed across the empty ground to the corner of the house. She paused to see if anyone had noticed an intruder, then cautiously stood to peek in the first window. A bedroom, just as she'd suspected, and empty. It didn't look as if anyone had used it for a long time.

The door to the living area was shut so she couldn't see anything else, but she was close enough now to catch the sound of an angry male voice. The words were indistinguishable.

She ducked down again and moved to the next window.

This one gave her a clear view of the open living area she'd expected to find.

What she saw brought her heart into her throat.

She took one good look, then ducked back down, out of sight, her thoughts racing.

Jerelski was there, and he was definitely angry. His back had been turned to her, but his whole body radiated an almost uncontrollable fury as he'd paced the floor in front of his two captives.

Tina Dornier was kneeling on the floor in front of the couch. She definitely looked frightened, but there'd been an alertness about her that made Maggie hope she'd be able to react intelligently to whatever was going to happen next.

What Maggie hadn't expected was the cringing figure huddled on the sofa that Tina was trying to comfort.

Grace Navarre. A drugged-out and badly battered Grace Navarre, if what little Maggie had seen was any indication.

That would definitely complicate things. On the other hand, Grace's presence complicated things for Jerelski, too. He had two possible hostages, but he also had two people who would be desperate to escape at the first opportunity.

Moving even more carefully than before, Maggie crept to the back door. Three rickety wooden steps led up to it, but she could still reach the knob from where she stood. And thank all the gods, it was unlocked.

Unfortunately, the door swung outward, not in,

but one of the first things they taught you when you were studying to be a cop was that you couldn't have everything your way. She would cope.

She would have to.

Scarcely breathing, she moved back to the window. There was no sign of Hoenig, but she had not the slightest doubt that he would be coming through that front door sometime in the next sixty seconds and to hell with whatever he'd been taught.

Back to the door. When he burst through the front door, she was a heartbeat behind him.

"Freeze!"

They both shouted the order. They both had their guns up and Jerelski in their sights.

And neither one of them moved fast enough to stop Jerelski from yanking Tina to her feet and around in front of him as a shield.

Maggie's heart stopped beating altogether.

Hoenig tightened his two-handed grip on his gun. His eyes had gone murderously black.

Jerelski shifted his grip, pulling Tina's arm up behind her until she cried out at the pain. He had a gun in his hand now, a small but undeniably deadly looking black gun. He pointed it at Fritz.

"Hoenig, isn't it? Fritz Hoenig?" he said. "We met at that conference in Denver a few months back. Remember?"

"Let her go, Jerelski. It's over. You can't gain anything by this."

"I don't think so," Jerelski said. "Not just yet."

Dragging Tina with him as a shield, he edged toward the front door.

Maggie's heart was pounding, but her grip on her gun was rock still and solid. Her mind was racing, weighing alternatives. There were several. None of them were good.

Rick's unarmed. Please, God, don't let him walk in on this.

She should have let him bring his pistol. She should have known that Hoenig's feelings for Tina would get in the way of his judgment. She should have grabbed a bullet-proof vest, and made Hoenig and Rick take one, too. She should have—

"Give it up, Jerelski," she said. "There are other officers out there in the trees. You can't get away, and there's no place to go even if you could."

"Actually, there is. You'd be surprised what comfortable arrangements can be made when you have a few million dollars to pay for them."

He was almost to the door. Tina stumbled, then whimpered and arched back in pain when he twisted her arm higher still. Her eyes were wide and swimming in tears, her body shaking, but in spite of everything, she hadn't given in to her fear.

Reluctantly, but without lowering his own gun, Hoenig backed up to give them more room.

"Oh, Fritz!" Tina cried. "I'm so sorry! I know you said I shouldn't leave the house, but—"

"It's all right, Tina," Hoenig soothed without taking his attention off Jerelski.

"I was in the trees. I was being really careful," Tina insisted tearfully. "*Really* I was! But I guess I was closer to the road than I thought because Grace spotted me and—"

Jerelski's thin lips curled in an ugly sneer. "Stupid bitch has her uses every now and then."

On the sofa, Grace groaned, then curled into a tighter ball. None of them paid her any attention.

"If either of you puts one foot out this door, I'll shoot you," Jerelski said. He took another step backwards to stand in the open doorway, Tina still held securely in front of him. His gaze flicked from Hoenig, who was closest, to Maggie, then back again. "I assure you, I'm a very good shot. I—"

The crack of a rifle cut off whatever he'd meant to say next. He arched back involuntarily, bringing his gun hand up, too, so that when he pulled the trigger, the bullet went in the ceiling, not Hoenig's heart.

Tina gasped, then jerked away. Jerelski tried to bring the gun up again, but couldn't. He staggered, shook his head as if trying to shake off a fly, then collapsed, face-down in a heap in front of the open door.

Only then could they see the large, cylindrical metal dart that was lodged in the muscles at the base of his neck.

A moment later, Rick stepped through the doorway, a rifle in his hand. He spared one glance for the unconscious man at his feet and another for his sister, who stared at him, then at Hoenig, then threw her arms around Hoenig's neck and collapsed, sobbing, on his chest.

Rick didn't seem to care. After that first glance, his gaze had riveted on Maggie.

Slowly, heart pounding, she lowered her gun.

"You all right?" he asked.

She nodded, but couldn't get any words out past a throat gone suddenly tight.

"Thank God!"

Maggie thought she'd never heard a more heartfelt prayer.

And then he stepped across Jerelski's body as if it were no more than a rug haphazardly tossed down on the floor. In three strides he was across the room. And then he wrapped her in his arms and kissed her and Maggie stopped thinking at all.

Grace was taken to the hospital. She would probably be there awhile. Between the drugs and Jerelski's battering, she was in pretty bad shape. Maggie suspected she would be forced into a drug treatment center after she was released from the hospital. With luck and a lot of help, maybe she'd eventually turn her life around. Maggie hoped so, though she wasn't planning to bet too much on the possibility.

Jerelski, too, was taken to the hospital, but he went under guard. As soon as the doctors confirmed he'd totally recovered from the effects of Rick's tranquilizing dart, he would be given a room at the jail courtesy of the town of Fenton.

Representatives from the police, DEA and District Attorney's office were already hard at work to make sure he wasn't granted bail. With all the material they'd found in Taublib's cabin, there was a good chance he'd eventually be granted a lifetime residence in Colorado's most secure prison.

Maggie wasn't interested in the details right now. Eventually, no doubt, she'd be dragged into the preparations for the trial. It was a hundred percent certainty she'd be required to testify. But all that was for the future.

Right now, the present was suddenly a whole lot more difficult to handle than she would have liked.

When Tina had refused to accept any medical treatment, the four of them—Rick, Hoenig, Tina and herself—had been brought to the Fenton police station. Rick's rifle and the tranquilizing dart he'd used had been confiscated and might be held as evidence in any inquiry. Given Grace's condition and Tina's testimony, Maggie suspected that there might not even be an inquiry, or that if there was, it would be no more than a formality.

Since she'd drawn her gun, too, Maggie knew she'd have a million forms and incident reports to fill out. Those could wait until tomorrow. Right now she was far too tired to string two coherent sentences together, let alone manage anything bigger.

Tina and Hoenig were off in some room somewhere, giving their statements. It would have been easier to pry George Washington off Mt. Rushmore than to have separated those two, so no one even tried. The last Maggie had seen them, they'd been sitting shoulder to shoulder, their hands laced together, heads bent and close so that no one else could catch their whispered, intimate conversation.

Maggie figured the wedding would be scheduled for the day after Tina's graduation next spring. She hoped she was invited.

She tried to tell herself it wasn't envy she was feeling, but she wasn't having much luck.

Those few, frantic minutes in the cabin and later, outside, had brought with them an entirely different perspective on life and on her life choices. They'd also driven a wedge of uncomfortable silence between her and Rick that had only grown wider and seemingly more unbridgeable with every passing hour.

After that wild, frantic kiss—a kiss, she realized now that had been driven as much by knee-wobbling relief as any deeper passion—they'd reluctantly pulled away from each other, and they'd been moving farther and farther away ever since.

She remembered the kiss. Most of the rest was a blur. The eventual arrival of their backup. Jerelski's arrest. The arrival of yet more police, then DEA agents who happily started an inch-by-inch search of the house even as they requested a warrant for a similar search of Jerelski's home, business and college office.

She and Rick had each given their statements. Separately, in separate rooms, to different recording clerks. Maggie didn't remember a lot about that, either.

They hadn't talked about what had happened. They certainly hadn't talked about how they felt about it. And they'd carefully avoiding meeting each other's gaze since they'd climbed into different squad cars for the ride back to town.

Bursey had been furious, of course, and roaringly delighted with Jerelski's capture. With luck, her boss would overlook all those rules and regulations she'd broken and just be happy with the fact that she and Rick and Hoenig had brought the man down. She might end up with a mild rebuke, maybe a single somber note in her next glowing evaluation, but that would probably be it.

There was even a small chance that she would end up with a commendation, maybe even a medal. One of the DEA agents had informed her there was a betting pool starting on which way it would go. He'd offered her a chance to join the pool. She'd declined. He hadn't believed her when she'd said she didn't care, one way or the other.

But she'd told the truth—reprimand or medal, she really *didn't* care which she got because either way, it really didn't matter.

What she cared about was Rick and what was starting to develop between them. No, what had already *exploded* between them, no matter how hard they'd tried to stop it.

What she cared about was this confusing tangle of feelings inside her. She didn't like being confused. She didn't like feeling lost, either. But right now, with Rick keeping his distance from her, she was *definitely* feeling lost.

And that was making her mad.

Just where did he get off *ignoring* her like this? How in the hell could he *possibly* pretend that just because they'd gotten Tina back, the rest of it, everything that had so quickly grown between them, no longer mattered?

She had a good mind to go over there and tell him so, too. At least then he couldn't just keep standing there, staring out that window as if she weren't even in the room.

Her increasingly angry thoughts were interrupted by the opening of the door.

For a moment, Bursey just stood there in the

open door eyeing both of them as if deciding which one he was going to rake over the coals first.

"You mind shutting the door?" Maggie snapped. "All that noise out there is annoying."

Bursey frowned, then shut the door and crossed the room to stand in front of her.

Maggie bristled. The last thing she wanted right now was another fight, but if Bursey wanted to fight...

"You want a job, Manion?"

Her jaw dropped. "I've got a job."

"Not with me. I can offer you less pay, fewer resources, the same long hours and the chance to fight with me on a regular basis." His grin was almost as startling as the offer. "How can you possibly resist?"

Work for Bursey? Stay in one place for more than a few months? Have a real home for a change, maybe learn to build a real life for herself? Make some friends who had absolutely nothing to do with her job? Go all out, maybe, and adopt a cat?

Her head spun at the thought. A week ago, she would have laughed at the thought. Now...

The yearning ache that started somewhere near her heart and rapidly spread outward caught her by surprise. Her stomach pitched. Her knees turned wobbly. And just like that, her anger vanished, replaced by utter wonder.

Beside her, she could hear Rick shift on his feet, but she didn't dare turn to look at him.

A job with Bursey? A home here in Fenton? The whole idea seemed absurd. Ludicrous. But she had to admit it had a certain appeal.

Was that what she wanted? A regular job? A regular life? Someone—well, some*thing* to come home to?

She'd never permitted herself to think about that sort of thing before, but now that Bursey had offered...

Colorado was a whole lot closer to Montana than Washington, D.C.

Maggie glanced at Rick. *Say something,* she pleaded silently.

He was watching her. She couldn't read the expression on his face, but she could *feel* the tension that suddenly gripped him.

Because of that tension in him, some of the tension in her eased. Her answer mattered to him. Really *mattered.* Which was crazy, because they hadn't known each other a whole three days.

Three days of arguing and worrying and running around trying to find a sister he hardly knew.

Three days of watching him move, watching him smile or frown or glare, and of knowing he was watching her.

Three days of being so aware of him that she would have known what he was doing, almost what he was thinking, just by closing her eyes and letting that awareness bleed through to her very bones.

A few hours of making love to him until they both nearly keeled over from the mind-blowing wonder of it.

As good as a lifetime, she thought.

Besides, she'd never been one to second guess what her own instincts told her to do.

"No, thanks," she said to Bursey. She deliberately didn't look at Rick when she said it. "I really appreciate the offer, but…no."

He actually looked a little disappointed, which was flattering, but not nearly flattering enough to make her change her mind.

"Oh," he said. He shrugged. "Well. I didn't really think you would, but it was worth a try."

He thrust out his hand. Maggie didn't hesitate to take it.

"You're a good officer, Manion. A real know-it-all pain in the butt, but a good officer. If you ever decide to you want to come back to Fenton…"

She smiled. "If I do, Chief, you'll be the first to know."

She waited until Bursey had shut the door behind him before she turned to face the silent man beside her.

He look tired, she thought, and realized with a surprise that it was late. Almost midnight, actually. The witching hour.

She'd never believed in ghosts or goblins or witches, but she wouldn't mind a little magic right about now. And a hefty shot of courage. Facing him like this, looking into his eyes, she realized, suddenly, just how much the next few minutes mattered.

"So you're going back to Washington." His voice sounded heavy, devoid of expression.

That was a good sign, she decided. Better than relief or, God forbid, downright cheerfulness.

"For a bit. I'll have to clean up a few things here, of course, but that shouldn't take long. Then Washington—" she was finding it a little difficult to breathe "—and after that, my next assignment."

He squared his shoulders, tried to look politely interested. His eyes had gone shadowed, though, and Maggie almost cheered from the relief that rushed through her at the sight.

"Another assignment?" he said. "Anywhere in particular?"

She moved closer. Close enough that he could grab her if he wanted.

"I was thinking…Montana."

His head snapped up as if she'd hit him. "Montana!"

Maggie smiled and leaned closer still. "That's what I was thinking. I figured it would be a nice change of pace, you know? It would have to be a university town, of course. I know a professor up there who chases grizzly bears for a living and—''

She didn't get a chance to finish because right about then he grabbed her and dragged her hard against him. And then he kissed her and she couldn't have gotten a word out if she'd tried.

She didn't really try.

* * * * *

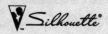

INTIMATE MOMENTS™

**A new generation begins
the search for truth in...**

A Cry in the Dark

(Silhouette Intimate Moments #1299)

by Jenna Mills

No one is alone....

Danielle Caldwell had left home to make a new life
for her young son. Then Alex's kidnapping rocked her
carefully ordered world. Warned not to call for help,
Dani felt her terror threatening to overwhelm her
senses—until tough FBI agent Liam Brooks arrived on
her doorstep, intent on helping her find Alex. Their
clandestine investigation led to a powerful attraction
and the healing of old wounds—and the discovery
of a conspiracy that could unlock the secrets of
Dani's troubled past.

The first book in the new continuity

FAMILY
SECRETS

THE NEXT GENERATION

Available June 2004 at your favorite retail outlet.

eHARLEQUIN.com

For **FREE online reading,** visit
www.eHarlequin.com now and enjoy:

Online Reads
Read **Daily** and **Weekly** chapters from
our Internet-exclusive stories by your
favorite authors.

Red-Hot Reads
Turn up the heat with one of our more
sensual online stories!

Interactive Novels
Cast your vote to help decide how these
stories unfold…then stay tuned!

Quick Reads
For shorter romantic reads, try our
collection of Poems, Toasts, & More!

Online Read Library
Miss one of our online reads?
Come here to catch up!

Reading Groups
Discuss, share and rave with other
community members!

For great reading online,
visit www.eHarlequin.com today!

INTONL

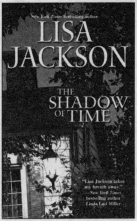
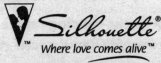

Gaining back trust is hard enough…but especially when you're being set up for murder!

USA TODAY bestselling author

MARY LYNN BAXTER

Divorce attorney Hallie Hunter can hardly keep her composure when Jackson Cole walks through her door, begging her to represent him in an ongoing murder investigation in which he's the prime suspect.

Never able to deny her ex-fiancé, Hallie is thrust toward a dangerous underworld as she helps him confront a devastating truth—and must decide for herself if she can ever live without him again.

WITHOUT YOU

"The attraction between the hero and heroine sparks fire from the first and keeps on burning hot throughout."
—*Publishers Weekly* on *Sultry*

Available in May 2004 wherever paperbacks are sold.

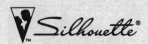
COMING NEXT MONTH

SIMCNM0504